DESTROY ALL CARS

BLAKE NELSON

Scholastic Press

New York

Excerpts from *Black Elk Speaks* © 2008 Suny Press Book. Reprinted by permission from
Suny Press.

Library of Congress Cataloging-in-Publication Data

Nelson, Blake
    Destroy all cars / Blake Nelson. – 1st ed.
        p. cm.
    Summary: Through assignments for English class, seventeen-year-old James Hoff
rants against consumerism and his classmates' apathy, puzzles over his feelings for his
ex-girlfriend, and expresses disdain for his emotionally distant parents.
    ISBN-13 978-0-545-10474-6 (hardcover : alk. paper)
    ISBN-10 0-545-10474-2 (hardcover : alk. paper)   [1. Social action – Fiction.
2. Consumption (Economics) – Fiction.   3. Ecology – Fiction.   4. Dating (Social
customs) – Fiction.   5. High schools – Fiction.   6. Schools – Fiction.   7. Family
problems – Fiction.]
    I. Title.

PZ7.N4328Des 2009
[Fic] – dc22

                                                                    2008034850

         10 9 8 7 6 5 4 3 2 1   09 10 11 12 13 14

                Printed in the U.S.A.   23
                First edition, May 2009

            The text type was set in Scala.
            Book design by Christopher Stengel

To James and Misha

Acknowledgments

Big thanks to Jodi Reamer and all the Writers House crew, Bethany Strout, Maja Nikolic, and Elena Santogade. Thanks to David Levithan and everyone at Scholastic. Also special thanks to my mom, who read a final draft; my sister Penny, who read early drafts; and especially Sally Cohen, who put the "On Nature" section up on her refrigerator when it looked like the book might never make it to print. Every time I saw "On Nature" on Sally's fridge, I thought, *I gotta finish that book....*

"Every generation needs a new revolution."
—*Thomas Jefferson*

PART
1

James Hoff
Junior AP English
Mr. Cogweiller
ASSIGNMENT: *four-page persuasive essay*

DESTROY ALL CARS!

We stand at the edge. We stand at the brink. We have come to a final point in history. Greenhouse gases are heating our oceans, choking our atmosphere, changing our entire planet. Toxins and pollutants threaten not only our lives, but all life on earth. If action is not taken, all will be lost!

We can no longer chip away at the edges of our problem with meaningless "feel good" solutions. Recycling, buying "green" products, Take the Bus to Work Day — none of these will save our atmosphere or slow down the disastrous heating effects of air pollution. Organic salad bars are not going to refreeze the North Pole. Instead we must fearlessly strike at the root of the problem.

We must destroy all cars.

We must destroy all cars for what they do.

We must destroy all cars for what they stand for.

We must destroy all cars to break the mind-set that makes it impossible to see beyond our own most immediate and selfish needs.

We must destroy all cars because if we don't, they will destroy us!

A world without cars is possible. But how can we imagine such a thing the way we live now?

PRIMITIVE MACHINE

The car is a primitive machine. It is not complicated. You put gas in it and poison comes out. It's pretty damn simple.

Is it a good idea to start your car in your garage and sit beside it, reading the paper, while your garage fills up with exhaust? No. Then why would that be a good idea on a global level?

I AM SO SICK OF CARS

I am sick of cars idling in my school parking lot. I am sick of the endless river of them that forms every morning on the main road by my house. I am sick of sitting on the bus and watching them packed all around me, ninety percent of them containing A SINGLE INDIVIDUAL. I am sick of that one woman sitting there in her cocoon of false safety, with her Poland Spring water and her Healthy Choice granola bar, polluting the world outside while inside, in her air-conditioned insulation pod, she deludes herself into thinking that drinking fake mineral water and eating fake candy bars is going to purify her body. I reject that person. I reject the falsity of this belief system.

THE LAMENESS OF PEOPLE IN GENERAL

I understand that people are lame and they cannot do without a luxury item once they possess it. I denounce their lameness.

I understand that people are weak and cannot walk to the mall once they have driven there. I denounce their weakness.

I understand that it is the nature of Consumer Americans to constantly drive their vehicles to different stores so they can buy endless amounts of useless crap. I denounce their simplicity of mind.

I understand that our entire economy is based on the production and consumption of USELESS CRAP. I denounce it all: TARGET, WAL-MART, ROSS DRESS FOR LESS, SEARS, MACY'S, KMART, MERVYNS. It is crap! All of it! Crap!

CALL TO ARMS

Young people, students, future citizens and leaders, I ask you to CLEARLY SEE where our present course is taking us. The automobile is the foundation upon which our unsustainable lifestyle is based. They must be DESTROYED. All of them. Even the cute ones. Even the little Mini Cooper that Daddy bought you for your birthday, Ashley.

Cars keep the present political system in place. They keep lower-class people going to war. They keep upper-class people in their mansions and their private jets.

By sitting in our gas-guzzling minivans in traffic, moving at three miles an hour, burning fuel pointlessly, we are keeping the whole car-based social system afloat. Every day OIL COMPANIES make BILLIONS of dollars because we lazy-ass Americans cannot ride a bike to school or work.

The End

January 17

Got a C+ on my essay. Typical. Cogweiller said it was too emotional and not supported by facts. Also he says calling people names is not an effective way to sway them to your point of view.

He wrote in the margin: *lazy-assed Americans.* Ha ha.

Sadie Kinnell wrote her paper about recycling and of course got an A. Cogweiller read hers out loud to his other class. That's what Gabe told me. I am not in Sadie Kinnell's AP English section, thank god.

January 18

Today at lunch, I saw Sadie Kinnell waiting in the food line. She's still hanging out with the annoying guy she supposedly broke up with, Will Greer. They were talking in line. It's unclear if they are officially broken up or not.

Sadie Kinnell was my girlfriend sophomore year. It was a complicated relationship. We fought a lot. We agreed about some things, though. She agrees that the destruction of the planet is bad. (Congratulations, Sadie!) However, we differ on what to do about it. For instance, she thinks "raising awareness" is a good strategy. Or wearing colorful bracelets that support causes like Forgiving Third World Debt or Helping the Refugees. She also started an Activist Club at our school, which is full of annoying do-gooder types. She's a priss, is what it boils down to. She gets really good grades and she'll probably go to an excellent college. But she couldn't kiss worth a crap. I don't even know why I'm talking about her now. She is meaningless.

Cogweiller says I can try again on the paper if I want a better grade. He says to use specific examples and to introduce a personal perspective.

James Hoff
Junior AP English
Mr. Cogweiller
MAKEUP ASSIGNMENT: *four-page persuasive essay*

THE CAR PROBLEM

We have a problem at our school. That problem is cars.

Every day when our school lets out, dozens of cars crowd into our school driveway. The line goes around the school and onto the highway and almost causes accidents. Then, for up to an hour, this caravan of over-size SUVs, Luxury Pickups, and Minivans idles in the driveway of our school, smothering us with exhaust and toxic emissions. Some of these vehicles are so large, their exhaust pipes are nearly at the same height as our freshmen's faces.

Breathe it in, boys and girls!

And this Is at a school where if you took one puff of a cigarette, you would be expelled for life. . . .

A SPECIFIC EXAMPLE:

My friend Gabe's mom picks him up in a Ford Expedition that sits so high up you need a smaller car to stand on in order to get into it. I asked him once what kind of gas mileage it gets. He didn't know. I told him to ask his mom, but she didn't know either. He said they fill it up once a week. It costs over a hundred dollars. His mom doesn't even look. I asked if his mom could at least turn the engine off while she's waiting. But Gabe says she can't turn it off because she gets too cold in the winter and she likes to keep the heat on. Or when it's summer, she gets too hot. She has to have climate control.

I'm like, I hope so. She's gonna need it WHEN WE ARE ALL FRYING FROM THE EFFECTS OF GLOBAL WARMING BECAUSE PEOPLE LIKE HER CAN'T TURN OFF THEIR STUPID CARS.

A PERSONAL PERSPECTIVE

As a young person, I think about environmental issues a lot. The main thing I think about is HOW WE ARE GREEDILY AND RECKLESSLY DESTROYING OUR PLANET. We are filling it with poison and waste because we are so lazy we cannot stop WALLOWING IN OUR CONSUMER AMERICAN CULTURE LONG ENOUGH TO STOP AND THINK ABOUT WHAT WE ARE DOING. People like Gabe's mother – who is perfectly nice, by the way – cannot imagine life without all the petty luxuries of the moment. She drives around, wasting gas, wasting everything she comes in contact with, *consuming* at a ridiculous rate, all because she has never had reason to stop and consider her lifestyle. She is a CONSUMER AMERICAN. She drives a car that gets THIRTEEN MILES TO THE GALLON. She goes to the mall EVERY DAY to buy USELESS CRAP, because that's all she knows to do. That's what the TV tells her to do. That's what the other moms do.

I am *so* not going to live here when I grow up. As soon as I graduate, I am MOVING TO OSLO. I went there once when I was thirteen. People there are much smarter than here. They don't even *have* Ford Expeditions. They're too big to fit on their roads.

The End

January 22

Went to see Cogweiller in his office. All that extra work, and all I got was a B–.

Cogweiller says that a "dramatic pose" is not as effective as "clear arguments and cogent rhetoric."

He thinks it's all a joke, that I'm goofing around, that I don't really mean what I'm saying.

Old people don't care what happens. They're done with the planet. They had their fun.

Cogs wanted to know what was up with all the capitalizations. I said, "That means I'm yelling."

He said, "Who are you yelling at?"

I said, "The world."

January 24

Cold and gloomy today. Dark when you leave for school, dark when you get home. And the sky is always gray. And then it rains all night.

This is not good for you, according to what we learned in biology last year about how lack of sunlight alters your mood and makes you depressed. Portland, Oregon, is one of the darkest places, too. It's a wonder we don't all kill ourselves.

Oh, wait, we already are.

January 25

In study hall today, Blaire Atwater decided to have a little
fun with me. She winked at her friend and then asked
me why I cut the elbows out of my sweater. I told her
that it makes the sweater look old, and that old sweaters
are cooler than new sweaters. She was like, "I don't
see why."

I said, "You wouldn't."

Then Mrs. Harris got mad and said I would have to
leave study hall if I couldn't shut up. I was like, why don't
you make *her* shut up? But Mrs. Harris thinks of me as a
troublemaker more than CONSUMER AMERICAN
Blaire Atwater. So I was identified as the at-fault person.

January 29

More idiocy regarding my sweater: A teacher stopped me
in the hall and asked me if my parents know that I
deface my clothing. That's the word he used, *deface*.
That's not even the right word.

That's nothing compared to the big display we had in
the front of school celebrating our "Aid to Victims of the
Hurricane," where they misspelled the words *separate* and
indomitable, and used the word *effect* wrong. School is not
a place to learn to spell. It is a place to learn to shop.

And no sooner did I escape my illiterate teacher than
I ran right into Will Greer. He avoided looking at me as
always. What must it be like to be Sadie's second
boyfriend? Sloppy seconds. Second in command. Second
place. He seems to like it. He'll settle for it anyway. He'll
take what he can get.

And then not ten minutes later I saw Sadie herself,
and several of the Activist Club members in the library.
They were all gathered around the back table, discussing
something, making posters it looked like, though I
couldn't see what they said. "Free the Chipmunks" or
something.

What a bunch of dorks.

James Hoff
Junior AP English
Mr. Cogweiller
ASSIGNMENT: *four-page essay on a person who has influenced you*

SADIE KINNELL: WORKING WITHIN THE SYSTEM

Sadie Kinnell is an activist who believes in working within the system. She believes in community action, working in groups, and getting people "on board." One example of her approach is that she thinks voting is a good way to change things. Of course we can't vote because we're in high school, but she accepts that. She says, "Why should we get to vote before we're eighteen and fully informed on the issues?"

I do not believe that anyone is fully informed on the issues. I don't think the system is set up to allow you to fully understand anything. I will not bore you with details, but take wars, for example. Does anyone ever fully understand why we are in them?

More issues I have with Sadie Kinnell:

1. Sadie Kinnell dresses terribly and thinks she is justified in doing so. She often said I was trying to shock people with my thrift-store clothes, which is kind of true, but what did she want me to do, go to Nordstrom and buy a Polo shirt? No, thank you.

2. The way we broke up was ridiculous, with her lecturing me on my attitude and my "nihilistic" worldview. That is so uncool.

3. Equally ridiculous: the fact that she was in *Willamette Week* as a "Person of Note." This happened because she helped the City Commissioner's Office raise money for a bike path along the river. It was so typical of Sadie. Looks good. Sounds good. Everyone loves a nice bike path. Everyone loves puppies, too. Meanwhile, polar bears are drowning because there is no ice and it's 122 degrees in India. What is a bike path going to do about that? Answer: nothing.

4. Sadie Kinnell is what people think of as "the solution." I have news for you: All Sadie Kinnell is going to do is shake hands with people and smile a lot and clean up little parks so that children can play in them safely. We don't need more parks for children. We need less cars. Less people. Less development. And we need it all lessened NOW.

5. The reality of what's happening to our planet is ... well ... the reality is unthinkable. That's why nobody thinks about it. Sadie sure doesn't.

6. Sadie Kinnell claims she did not like Will Greer when she broke up with me. I find this hard to believe. They were always talking in chem, according to my

friend Gabe. Gabe even said he felt there was "something going on" between them. Personally – though I still consider Will to be annoying – I am not terribly offended by this. Sadie and I were having serious problems. Sadie thought I should go on antidepressants. When she said that, I knew it was over. She was no longer seeing me for who I was. I do not need antidepressants.

7. Still, it is important to note that Sadie recommended medication. The world is in serious danger, and the solution? Pills. Drugs to make you not think about it. In CONSUMER AMERICA, thinking about things is as bad as not buying useless crap. It is counterproductive. Mental accuracy is a bad thing. Reality is meaningless. If you see clearly, if you express yourself clearly, you become the problem. *Your bad attitude is not helping.*

8. I denounce the do-gooders, the feel-gooders, the "activist clubs," and anyone else who makes people feel like the problem is being taken care of. Trust me. The problem is *not* being taken care of. Look outside your window. What do you see? Cars. Millions of them. They are the problem. And they aren't going anywhere.

The End

February 1

Went to see Cogweiller in his office. He was not happy.
He gave me the evil eye for thirty-seven seconds. I think
that's a record.

Then he gave me back my paper. On the bottom was
written:

- no more numbers or lists in my essays.
- no more writing about other students.
- no more insulting people or using derogatory
  language.
- no more subheadings or other manifesto stylings.

Cogs wouldn't even give me a grade. He said I had to
do it over. Still, I liked that he called it *manifesto stylings*.
He actually wrote that. Which is rad.

DISCO BOWLING

Went bowling with Gabe on Friday night. We were
meeting a girl named Renee, who Gabe likes. He wanted
me to be his wingman. Though I do not possess
extensive "wingman" skills, I agreed to go.

Gabe's mom drove us there in the Ford Expedition. I
felt like an evil warlord sitting in the back of it, looking
down on smaller, more fuel-efficient cars. I said nothing,
though. Gabe checked his cell phone for any further
communications from Renee. There were none.

We walked into the bowling alley. It was noisy and it
smelled like socks. People were running around, talking
on their cells, giggling about whatever, drinking diet
soft drinks.

We found Renee. She was with two other girls and
two boys I didn't know. They were typical high school
students of suburban extraction. The girls wore Nikes
and low-rise jeans and hoodies. They conducted themselves like CONSUMER AMERICANS, chewing gum
and talking about recent purchases and what brands of
beauty products they preferred. The boys were the
same — T-shirts, skate-shoes with the laces tucked in,
baggy jeans.

Gabe asked Renee what was up. Not much was. They
were about to start bowling.

Gabe and I changed into our bowling shoes. Renee
tried to start the automatic scorer. It wouldn't come on,
so she pushed a button that summoned the man at the

front desk. This man was a very large person with a mullet. Also his pants didn't fit, so we saw his ass crack when he leaned over the scoring table. Everyone thought this was the funniest thing they had ever seen. Especially the boys. "Did you see that guy's ass crack!?" they kept saying. Har har har. It became the running joke of the night.

In case anyone is wondering what I looked like, I was at that moment wearing brown polyester slacks, a tan shirt, and my black sweater that has the elbows cut out. I also had black socks on and some old white deck shoes I found at Salvation Army. I also don't shampoo my hair, which is long and hangs partially in my face. In short, I looked like a total freak by the standards of other CONSUMER AMERICANS. I visited Oslo a couple years ago. I fit in better there. In my own country I look like an alien.

Also, in case anyone else is wondering, my own family is not particularly ecologically aware. In fact, my dad is one of the worst polluters ever. He never met a combustion engine he didn't like. My all-time favorite Dad story is the time he took a generator with us camping in Arizona. For an entire weekend he ran a gas engine, in the woods, to charge his computer and watch his little TV. It was hilarious. And terribly sad. My sister, Libby, tried to get him batteries for the TV so we wouldn't have to listen to the generator running all night but he wouldn't.

"Batteries run out. Gas engines never run out," he told my sister. He actually said that.

Back at the bowling alley: Once the automatic scoring thing was fixed, we were good to go. We all typed our names in. Gabe and I tried to find bowling balls. We walked around looking at the different colors and sizes.

Gabe considered many different balls. He was worried that if he didn't choose the right one, Renee wouldn't like him as much. "Does this one look too girly?" he asked. "Are the black ones cooler than the ones with swirlies?"

This is the typical fallacy on which all of CONSUMER AMERICA is based. Some piece of useless crap will make people like you.

We started our game. The first girl up was Renee's little sister, a freshman. She ran forward and threw her bowling ball into the air. THUNK. The ball smashed painfully onto the wood and bounced and rolled into the gutter. Gabe and I looked at each other. Freshmen are pretty funny.

She didn't care, though. As soon as she was done, she got on her cell phone and started telling her friend about a rash someone had in her gym class. *What do you think it was? . . . I don't know. . . . It was all red . . . and bumpy . . . and sort of . . . gooey.*

Gabe elbowed me. My turn. I stood and found my ball. Everyone watched me and I began to feel self-conscious. I took my place and stared down the polished corridor at my objective, the ten pins lined up in a tri-angle. This was the moment I realized that it was Disco Bowling night. I realized this because I saw a sign above our lane that said:

EVERY FRIDAY IS
DISCO BOWLING NIGHT!
10PM to 2AM

Wow. Disco Bowling. I checked my watch. It was almost ten. We were in luck.

But it wasn't Disco Bowling yet, and I still had to take my turn. I walked forward, swung the ball back, swung it forward, let it go . . . but just like the freshman girl, my release was a half second late. The ball went too high. THUNK. It bounced twice and piddled into the gutter.

"My ball holes were sticky," I explained to the group. The boys laughed. Sort of. The girls looked at me funny. They could sense I was holding myself apart from them. Which was true. I didn't mean to. It's just that I don't know what to say to people like them. No one wants to hear about my doomsday scenarios. And I don't want to talk about ass cracks.

"Dude, what happened?" Gabe whispered when I sat down. This was uncalled for, since I did get four pins on my second roll.

"Dude, whattaya mean?" I said back. "I got a four. Let's see you get a four."

Gabe stood up. It was his turn now. I called him "dude" a couple more times to annoy him. Then I sat back.

He got a six.

We got through our first game. Everyone settled in. Then one of Renee's friends came over and sat beside me. Her name was Stephanie.

STEPHANIE: So what's your deal?

ME: What do you mean?

STEPHANIE: You're sitting here by yourself. You're not talking to anyone.

ME: I'm shy.

STEPHANIE: You know what they say. Shyness is a form of vanity.

ME: Really?

STEPHANIE: Sure. Shy people are trying to bring attention to themselves. But in a negative way.

ME: I didn't know that.

STEPHANIE: Doesn't it make sense, though? If a person won't hang out, isn't that sort of vain?

ME: Maybe so. Who said that, anyway? Is that from the Bible?

STEPHANIE: It's probably from somewhere. What happened to your sweater?

ME: Nothing. I cut the elbows out.

STEPHANIE (*looking at the elbow holes*): That's weird. Are you in Drama Club?

ME: No. It's just a thing I do. It makes the sweater look old. It makes it look like I've had it so long the elbows have worn out.

STEPHANIE: But you haven't, though.

ME: I know. It's just this thing I do.

STEPHANIE (*sighing*): I guess some people just have to be different.

ME: So what about you? What's your deal?

STEPHANIE (*relieved to be talking about herself*): Oh, nothing much. I go to school. I hang out with my friends. You know. . . .

ME: Huh.

STEPHANIE: What else? Ummmm. I like to party.

ME: Yeah. A lot of people like to party.

STEPHANIE: And I like to, you know, do stuff . . . and chill, and listen to music. And just . . . hang out, basically. . . .

ME: That is really interesting.

STEPHANIE: I'm more of a stop-and-smell-the-roses type of person. Aren't you?

ME: Pretty much. Yeah. I'm a smeller.

STEPHANIE: I mean, I feel like, why get all worked up about stuff if you don't have to? You know?

ME: Yup.

STEPHANIE (*as the lights are dimmed*): Oh no. What's that? Why are they turning down the lights?

ME: I think it's time for Disco Bowling.

STEPHANIE: What's that?

ME: See that big sign over there that says Disco Bowling?

STEPHANIE: Yeah?

ME: That's what it is.

At that point Disco Bowling officially began. They dimmed the lights, put on some Bee Gees, turned on the sparkle ball. It was like being in the seventies, in a disco, except nobody was dancing, and there was bowling. Actually, Renee and Stephanie danced between their turns. They did the ride-the-pony dance, turning little circles in place. I think that's supposed to represent a sexual act, but I'm not sure. They were ignoring Gabe and me at this point. Gabe didn't look too good. He was doing his hangdog thing. Poor Gabe. He never gets what he wants. Who does?

When it was time to go, Renee barely said good-bye. Gabe and I ended up standing alone in front of the bowling alley. His mother came and picked us up in the Ford Expedition.

We pulled out of the parking lot. The Ford Expedition, by the way, has a huge metal battering ram on the front in case you need to punch through any walls or blockades or any other man-made barriers on the way home from the bowling alley. It also has little metal grates around the signal lights, in case rioting strip-mall goers decide to attack you with baseball bats while you're signaling a left turn. All that extra weight, of course, burns huge amounts of extra gasoline.

In the darkness of the backseat, I asked Gabe how it went with Renee.

"You saw it," he mumbled. "She barely talked to me."

I nodded sympathetically.

"You could have helped a little more," he said. "You could have been a better wingman."

"I'm sorry," I said. And I was.

James Hoff
Junior AP English
Mr. Cogweiller
MAKEUP ASSIGNMENT: *four-page essay on a person who has influenced you*

THE IMPORTANCE OF MOMS

Mothers are an important influence on their children and the other kids in the neighborhood. Take my friend Gabe's mom. She is a nice mom. Gabe likes her. The other kids like her. I like her. On the surface she appears perfectly normal. She reads Oprah books and waits in line at Starbucks and has a purple Patagonia fleece she wears every day. But if anything goes wrong, she dissolves into tears and panic. She is deeply afraid of the world. That's why she has fourteen credit cards and drives a Ford Expedition with a two-hundred-pound metal grate on the front. Because they protect her.

Then there's Rich Herrington's mom. She is the hot mom of our group. Apparently, among any group of high school boys, there is always a "hot mom." Mrs. Herrington plays her part. She wears a sexy bathing suit at the pool, which definitely looks good on her. She is not like Gabe's mom, who is just trying to survive another day. Mrs. Herrington wants to look like the latest celebrities on TV or the cheerleaders at school. She consumes vast amounts of USELESS CRAP that she thinks will keep her young and desirable. Of course that is not actually possible, but that doesn't stop her from buying the USELESS CRAP. Which is good for the economy. And good for the boys around the pool.

There's another mom down the street everyone calls "the punk rock mom." She wears tight black jeans and checked Vans. She and her husband have a girl who is in eighth grade. They enrolled her in all these special programs for the "gifted" or the "artistic" or whatever. That can't be good. Gabe tried to talk to her once and she just ran off. She dresses sort of punk rock herself but she isn't that into it. It must be embarrassing to have parents who are trying to be cool all the time. We saw her crying once while she was riding her bike. She's gonna be a total mess in high school.

My mom is one of the better moms. *I* like her, anyway. She grew up in Tucson, Arizona. She started to go to medical school, but then she met my dad. Now she manages a medical supply business. I don't know how my dad got with her. He's a bonehead. My mom's smart and pretty chill about stuff. Even when we disagree, we understand each other. Still, I don't talk to her as much as I used to. When my dad left, we got closer. And my little sister, Libby, too. The three of us rallied around each other. But then Dad came back and there was a new distance between Mom and me. That was because my mom had to spend more time on him. And kiss his butt.

My friend Jessica Carlucci's parents are the smartest of all my friends'. Her dad is an architect and makes houses out of alternative materials with solar panels and non-detergent washing machines. Jessica's mom does yoga and eats organic food. Jessica's parents are the only grown-ups I've met who seem to know what's up. But when you look at them closely, most of it is just surface. Like her dad has a garage full of useless luxury items, along with a full arsenal of the same gas-powered crap my dad has. Their gardener soaks their lawn every week with poisons and chemicals to get it just the right shade of green. And her mom, too; beneath the yoga exterior, what is there? She shops at Nordstrom. She buys plastic water bottles by the case. She never thinks about how much jet fuel she's using when she's flying around doing her consulting business.

Does being smarter and a little more aware do anything? Does it change anything? No. I never say this to Jessica, though. She's sensitive about her family because her dad had an affair when she was little and their family almost broke up. So there's a "no talking about anything" policy in their house. Everything is FINE.

The End

February 6

Wow. I never got a D before. It felt kind of liberating. You can only go up from a D.

Cogs didn't look too well today. I hope he's feeling all right. He stood over me for several seconds when we got our papers back, giving me the Cogweiller stare.

After school I asked if I could do another makeup. He strongly encouraged me to do so.

February 7

Hung out with Jessica Carlucci after school. We went to the gym to watch her sister's JV basketball game. Jessica was talking about college stuff. All the smart kids are thinking about college stuff now.

Last year when I broke up with Sadie, Jessica helped me a lot. That was the period when we changed from knowing each other to becoming actual friends. I wonder why we never went out. She does seem to like me. I'm not sure why. Because I understand her, I guess. I don't judge her. I don't know *why* I don't judge her. I judge everybody else.

Jessica is very pretty. And she wears really nice clothes and earrings and gets her hair done and all that. She'll marry some good-looking rich guy someday. That's what I thought as I watched the girl basketball players fall over each other chasing a loose ball. And she'll live in the West Hills and take her kids to tennis lessons at the club. She will grow up to represent everything I hate.

But you know what? Jessica Carlucci was the only one who understood what it did to me to break up with Sadie. Nobody else got it. Nobody else understood. She used to call me late at night, to see if I was okay.

So there you go.

James Hoff

Junior AP English

Mr. Cogweiller

MAKEUP TO THE MAKEUP ASSIGNMENT: *four-page essay on a person who has influenced you*

KARL MARX

One person who has influenced me is Karl Marx. He was a revolutionary and the first Marxist (duh), and an important thinker who has influenced people around the world.

Karl Marx was alive during the Industrial Revolution, when the first factories were being invented. He looked around and saw that poor people were going to have to work in the factories, and he realized that the men who ran the factories were going to take advantage of the poor people, like make them work twelve hours a day and make little kids work and just generally screw them over in every way possible. It was a very bad situation and it was only going to get worse.

So Marx got involved.

Actually, he didn't get involved. He went to the library and read a lot of books and let his hair grow so that when he became famous he would look distinguished and have a huge beard like other notable philosophers.

Anyway, after he read a lot of books, he wrote *The Communist Manifesto,* which is awesome and one of my favorite books.

The Communist Manifesto tells all those poor people to get together, not take any crap from the factory owners, and fight back. There's some philosophy and other complicated stuff, too, so that people can study it in college and write books about it.

The main thing I like about Marx is all those years he spent hanging around the library. Whenever I'm at the Central Library downtown and I see homeless people wearing pots on their heads or talking to newspaper boxes, I think: *That might be the next Karl Marx.*

Or maybe I am the next Karl Marx. Because I spend a lot of time thinking about the evils of the world and wandering around the public libraries. Also, as soon as I can, I'm going to grow a huge beard because huge beards are rad.

The End

February 11

Yes! This is what Cogs wrote on the bottom of my essay:

You are not Karl Marx. And you need a conclusion to this essay. But good explanation of Marxist ideas. B+

I can't believe it. B+! I'm getting to him. The Cogster!

PART
2

February 12

Will and Sadie broke up. They've broken up before, but now it's definitely over. It's official. I guess all the Activist Girls were talking about it before school. Jessica gave me the full update.

It's always bugged me that I didn't get a new girlfriend and Sadie got Will. It seemed so like her to get with someone right away. And so like me not to.

To be honest, the news kinda weirded me out. After school I walked with Gabe to Fred Meyer's where we wandered the aisles like we do. We went into the sports section and threw the nerf football around. Then we played some frisbee golf. I couldn't stop thinking about Sadie. It's hard to imagine her without a boyfriend. I don't know why exactly. It's not like I care what she does.

When I finally got home, dinner was almost ready. I ran upstairs really fast to check if Sadie had designated herself as single on her Facebook page. She had. Wow. That was interesting. She had a bunch of new friends, too. Twenty or so, since I last looked. Some of these were older activist types. People she met doing her bike path project. A lot of them were guys, I noticed. Had she gone out with any of them? What if she'd had sex with one of them?

Yikes.

That was the other big thing about Sadie and me — we never had sex. I always pretend that I wanted to and she didn't, but that's not really true. Gabe says she would have, if I'd made a big deal about it. We were just too young, really. We were sophomores. We were clueless.

Downstairs, my mother kept yelling for me to come to dinner. My dad finally came up and knocked on the door. I was to come now and eat "with the family." I was like, okay, okay, and I went downstairs and sat there and ate "with the family." Like that means anything.

Fortunately, Libby talked the whole time about some girl at her school who had a rash. I mentioned that I had met another freshman girl who had a rash. Thus I participated in the conversation "with the family."

After dinner I still felt restless and weird. I tried a little Spanish homework but that was not happening. So I hopped on my bike and rode down to Shari's, the local 24-hour restaurant, and drank a bunch of coffee and wrote a bunch of crap in my notebook.

But that didn't help. When I rode back, it was misting and cold and not the best bike-riding weather. Back home, I went online again and checked Sadie's page to see if she'd added anything new in the last three hours. She hadn't. She obviously has better things to do than waste time on the internet . . . unlike me, who spent an hour and a half doing this:

THE ONE TRUE YOU – A Survey
Name:
James Hoff

Age:

17

Birthplace:

Portland, Oregon

Current Location:

Upstairs, in bedroom, at computer, 11:52 p.m.

High School:

Evergreen High School: Home of The Fighting Owls! (?)

Eye Color:

Black (from seeing the future)

~~Hair~~ Lung Color:

Black (from breathing the air of the future)

Height:

5'11"

Right Handed or Left Handed:

Right

Your Heritage:

CONSUMER AMERICAN

The Shoes You Wore Today:

White deck shoes. I love them. They are the only thing I love.

Your Weakness:

Robots, girls, girl robots.

Your Fears:
That dumb people are happier than I am; that clueless people have more fun.

Your Perfect Pizza:
Canadian bacon with pineapple

Goals You Would Like To Achieve This Year:
1) Overthrow petroleum-based world economic order;
2) Have sex

Your Most Overused Phrase On an Instant Messenger:
WTF

Thoughts First Waking Up:
How much longer will our travesty of a civilization last?

Your Best Physical Feature:
Pointing finger.

Your Bedtime:
When I can't take it anymore.

Your Most Missed Memory:
Being so young I did not understand what was happening to the world.

Pepsi or Coke:
Is that a choice?

McDonald's or Burger King:
For what? Killing yourself?

Lipton Iced Tea or Nestea:
You're joking.

Chocolate or Vanilla:
Shut up.

Tea or Coffee:
Nobody cares!

Do you Smoke:
I don't but I might as well.

Do you Sing:
I scream pretty damn good.

Do you Shower Daily:
I scrub the sickness of my species off myself every day. It always comes back.

Have you been in Love:
It took you long enough. Yes, I have been in love. Now ask me some questions about it. And how about some questions about sex?

Do you want to go to College:
I thought these quizzes were supposed to be about sex? And dating. And girls. I want to answer questions about my love life and if I like long walks on the beach and what my favorite color is. Then I want you to calculate my "score" or my "type" and tell me what kind of girl I should be with and preferably arrange a meeting with her so that I don't have to leave my room.

Also some pictures of that (or any) girl in various states of undress would be nice.

Do you want to get Married:
Married? I haven't even got laid yet! What is your problem? These tests are supposed to be fun! It said right on the top: "For amusement purposes only."

Do you believe in yourself:
That is the only thing I believe in.

Do you think you are Attractive:
I am a certain type. If you like that type, you'll like me.

Are you a Health Freak:
In a way.

Do you get along with your Parents:
I do not waste my time fighting with my parents, who are typical CONSUMER AMERICANS. They don't understand me, anyway. I never ask for the car. I never ask for money. What's wrong with me? I wear old clothes that I buy myself. I must be mentally ill. That's how my parents think, all right? They are not worth talking about, and they are definitely not worth fighting with. What would be the point?

Do you like Thunderstorms:
Yes! And there are going to be a lot of them in the future, so I am in luck! There will also be more hurricanes, tornadoes, heat waves, and other "unusual" weather patterns because we're filling the

atmosphere full of ungodly chemicals. "Gee," we say as we sit in our CO2-spewing SUVs, "what's up with the weird weather?"

Do you play an Instrument:
Only when I consume certain gaseous combustibles.

In the past month have you Drunk Alcohol:
Bud Light, (burp) every chance I git.

In the past month have you Smoked:
Marlboro Reds, (cough) ever chance I git.

In the past month have you been on Drugs:
Spark a bowl (cough cough hacking cough) every chance I git.

In the past month have you gone on a Date:
With my hand! Har har har!

In the past month have you eaten a box of Oreos:
Oreos are irrelevant to everything that I stand for. But I like them. And I consume them on occasion.

In the past month have you eaten Sushi:
Sushi is from Japan. The important thing to know about Japan is that their robot technology is far advanced over ours. This is a national disgrace. When it is 200 degrees on the face of the earth and all the people are

dead, the Japanese robots will be sipping iced drinks in their shady palaces while our feeble American robots fan them with palm leaves.

What is your favorite TV Show:
Nova, Discovery Channel, anything with robots in it.

What is your Favorite Band:
Ima Robot

What is your Favorite Movie:
I, Robot

What is your Favorite Book:
The Robot Manifesto

In the past month have you been Dumped:
Depends on what you mean by dumped. Do you mean emotionally devastated by the sudden withdrawal of love by someone you totally trust and depend on? Do you mean sent into a death spiral of mental anguish by your soulmate tearing herself away from you without warning? Do you mean your whole world collapsing all around you, to the point where you don't care if you're alive or dead? No, I have not been dumped.

In the past month have you gone Skinny Dipping:
I denounce lame attempts at "rebellion" that serve only to maintain the current system. Why? Is somebody going?

In the past month have you Stolen Anything:
Stealing implies possession. I denounce possession. However, I have on occasion moved certain objects from one place to another.

Ever been Drunk?
The only people in America who haven't been drunk are people who don't own television sets. To these people I say: Go to the store, buy a TV, turn it on. Observe how the people in Bud Light commercials act. Now imitate these people: Dress like a "slacker," drive your humorously feeble vehicle to a convenience store, buy some Bud Light, and drink it. Notice that sickening feeling in your stomach? Feel that wooziness in your head? That is drunkenness. You are now drunk.

Ever been called a Tease:
What?

Ever been Beaten Up:
Yes. I considered it an honor.

Ever Shoplifted:
Why would I have to shoplift? My parents are CONSUMER AMERICANS. They bring home carloads of useless crap every day.

How do you want to Die:
From natural causes. Not because of other people's greed and stupidity.

What do you want to be when you Grow Up:
Alive.

Number of Drugs I have taken:
72 aspirin, 37 Tylenol, 48 Advil (to ease the pain)

Number of CDs I own:
76, not counting Bob Dylan's "Masterworks," which my dad insisted on buying me for Christmas. Thanks, Dad.

Number of things in my Past I Regret:
One. Falling in love with Sadie Kinnell. But no. I don't regret it.

No, I don't regret my time with Sadie. To be honest, it was probably the best thing that ever happened to me.

The problem is what's happened after. In the last nine months my life has gone pretty much straight downhill. I don't even feel like myself anymore. I go to school. I eat lunch. I feel like I'm watching everything through glass. When I try to talk to other girls, I'm having a whole other conversation with myself at the same time. Talking is a waste, anyway. No one actually hears what you say. They just start talking themselves, saying irrelevant, pointless things that I already know or don't need to know. And then I get pissed off when I don't have anything to do on Friday night. The only time I can make sense of anything is when I write it down. But you can't show up at keg parties with a laptop.

It's so weird that Sadie's single again, that she's *out*

there again. I can feel this tingle in the air, like she's *right there*, like she might be sitting in her room typing something at this exact moment, or lying in her bed, or downstairs having warm milk in her kitchen.

I can feel her presence. I can see her perfectly in my mind. Sadie. She is out there. And she is free.

February 17

Went downtown yesterday to the Central Library so I
could get some Russian stuff for my World History class.
I gathered an armload of books and camped out in the
main reading room.

Then, coincidence of coincidences, who walks in?
Sadie Kinnell. At first I thought she was with Will
because I thought I heard his annoying dork voice, but it
wasn't him. She was by herself. I was at a back table, and
she didn't see me, so I slid down in my chair and hid
behind *The Bolshevik Revolution: A Pictorial Account.*

Sadie and I used to hang out at the downtown library
a lot. It was one of our favorite things to do when we first
started going out. We'd sit around talking and not doing
our homework. Then we'd get coffees across the street at
Café Artiste and talk more. She was big into animal
rights then. I was into existentialism, *The Stranger,*
anything involving cool French dudes with slicked-back
hair and cigarettes.

Anyway, so there I am, hiding behind *The Bolshevik
Revolution* and sneaking looks across the room. Of
course Sadie can't quietly look something up on the
computer. She has to go right up to the reference person
and announce herself. The library information guy
stares up at her with his thick glasses. Sadie is a people
person. Why get it done in half the time on the computer
when you can interact with a fellow human and impress

him with your earnest caring, plus maybe someday he will vote for you when you run for president? Sadie used to say there was something special and important about every person on the earth. I was like, yeah, they are all taking the place of a salmon or a bear or one of the other animals we have driven to extinction.

Sadie and thick glasses guy start chatting and researching and bonding. Everyone bonds with Sadie Kinnell. When he's done everything one human can possibly do for another, she thanks him sincerely and goes upstairs to continue her search. I watch her go. Meanwhile, thick glasses guy goes back to his desk, all smiles. He's totally in love with her. It can happen that quick.

I sit there, watching all of this, slunk down in my chair, gazing over the top of my book. The room is still electric with the presence of Sadie, even after she's gone. I look at the clock. I look at my stuff. What should I do? Go find her? Sit here? Pretend I don't know she's somewhere above me, in the same building I'm in?

Before I can stop myself, I get up and grab my coat and backpack. I'm going upstairs to see what she's doing. Maybe I'll pretend I'm looking for something myself. Or maybe I'll spy on her. Or maybe I'll hide in the bathroom.

I sneak up the stairs, creeping slowly, watching above me. When I make it to the second floor, I stash my stuff in the Art and Music Room and peek across the hallway at the Social Sciences and Government Room, where I'm sure she is. I think for a second. What am I doing exactly? I'm not sure. I screw up my courage and go for it anyway. I tiptoe across the hall.

The periodical shelf is by the door, so I go there first. I grab a copy of *Psychology Today*. I open it and pretend to read. I scan the room. I don't see Sadie. But I listen for a minute and I hear her in the bookshelves. She's mumbling to herself like she does sometimes. "B . . . B . . . here we go . . . B . . . B-E . . . B-E-A . . . okay, that's it . . . Charles Beatty . . . Douglas Beatty . . ." It sort of kills me how she does things like that. Cute, weird things. She really was the perfect girl for me. At least on a cuteness/weirdness level.

I listen and figure out exactly where she is. I think about sneaking up behind her, maybe surprising her somehow, or *shushing* her, or something funny like that. But would that be funny? Or creepy? She isn't my girlfriend anymore. We aren't, technically, even friends.

I decide to bail. It's a terrible feeling. To be that close to someone and then realize you have no access. You are not in her life. Not at all. I put *Psychology Today* back and duck out of the room. I run back to Art and Music, where I hide behind some Elton John CDs.

James Hoff
Junior AP English
Mr. Cogweiller
ASSIGNMENT: *personal reflection on a place or location*

REFLECTIONS ON THE MALL

I love the rumor that the air in malls is oxygen enriched to make you stupid and make you buy stuff. Why are you there if you're not stupid and going to buy stuff?

I love watching people at the mall. Junior high girls shuffling around, chewing gum, flipping their hair, their cells stuck to the sides of their faces. *Oh mah gawd!* they say into their phones, as their pea-sized brains struggle to comprehend the food court.

Then the boys, in their camo cargo shorts, Old Navy tees, backward baseball caps. Checking out the girls. Checking out the new PlayStation. Checking out the Spicy Chicken Wraps at California Kitchen. They have curly blond locks, pucca shell necklaces. Remarkably, they are still wearing shorts and Vans slip-ons, in February. Why not? It is a controlled environment here at the mall. The temperature is our bitch, *bitch.*

And the moms, overloaded with shopping bags and babies and other burdens. Despite their armloads of crap, they buy still more crap: Bed, Bath & Beyond crap. Crate & Barrel crap. Pottery Barn crap. Then a quick stop at Starbucks, or Ben & Jerry's for a shot of sugar to keep them going (buying).

Dads, too, sometimes appear at the mall, though they always look a little lost, surrounded by non-environment-destroying knickknacks. Maybe there's something useful for Dad down at Sears. There must be some sort of gas-powered machinery there. Maybe something to poison the lawn. Or amputate tree limbs. Or exterminate mice and other small animals who dare to co-exist in our living spaces.

People do what they are programmed to do. People are button-pushing robots.

Their alarm clocks wake them up. They push a button to shut them off. They go into their bathrooms and crap and piss. They push a button to eliminate their waste. They enter their kitchens groggy and hungry. They push buttons and food and caffeine products appear.

They enter their garage areas and insert themselves into their vehicles. They push buttons to adjust the interior climate, the comfort level of their seats, the angle of the steering wheel. Then they start the car and push a button to open the garage door. On the street, they push a button on their GPS unit and it tells them where to go. *Take the next left.*

At the mall they push a button and enter the automated parking garage. There they leave their vehicles and, if they are unlucky, HAVE TO EXPOSE THEMSELVES TO NATURE FOR A FEW SECONDS, until they are safely inside Nordstrom. They proceed, quickly pushing buttons on their communication devices and attaching them to the sides of their faces so they can communicate with other button-pushing robots.

The button-pushing robots then proceed through the oxygen-enriched air, which refuels them and primes them for their primary purpose: buying useless crap. They proceed fully loaded with credit cards, debit cards, Mileage-Plus cards. They go into the stores. They evaluate the selections. What shall they buy today? Useless gadgets? Ugly shirts? Something made of plastic? They move silently across the polished marble floors. They shuffle. They consume. They touch base. Then they return to their vehicles.

You think I'm kidding, don't you? You think I'm joking. People aren't robots. It's just a little riff I'm doing. Having a little fun. WELL, GO TO THE MALL AND LOOK AT THE PEOPLE. LOOK AT THEIR FACES AND TELL ME THEY HAVE REAL THOUGHTS. TELL ME THEY KNOW WHAT IS HAPPENING TO THE WORLD AND THEY ARE CAPABLE OF THINKING SOMETHING THEY WERE NOT TOLD TO THINK BY THEIR TVS OR THEIR COMPUTERS OR THE COMMUNICATION DEVICES STUCK TO THE SIDES OF THEIR FACES. PEOPLE REALLY ARE ROBOTS. THEY REALLY ARE. I DON'T CARE WHAT ANYONE SAYS. THEY ARE.

THE END
[not handed in]

February 17 (continued)

So I'm hiding among the Elton John CDs, in the Art and
Music Room, and when I look up, there she is. Sadie.
She's spotted me.

SADIE: James! Oh my God! Is that you?
ME: Uh . . .
SADIE: What are you doing here?
ME: ——
SADIE: I didn't know you still came to the library.
ME: Uh, yeah . . . sometimes . . .
SADIE: What are you looking at? CDs? They got
    anything good?
ME: Not really.
SADIE (*looking around at the Art and Music Room*):
    I never come in here. It's nice.
ME: ——
SADIE: It's so weird I ran into you. What are you
    doing these days?
ME: Not too much.
SADIE: I always mean to say hi at school. I just . . .
    it feels awkward . . . and Will always got a little
    weird about it.
ME: Yeah? Why?
SADIE: I don't know. He got jealous sometimes.
    And he hates it if I mention you. I figured it
    would be best to . . . you know . . .

ME: Never talk to me again?

SADIE: No. Not at all. But you know. Boys get jealous.

ME: I guess so.

SADIE: So what about you? How are things? Are you still writing?

ME: A little.

SADIE: You never joined the school paper, I noticed.

ME: No.

SADIE: That seems like such a waste. You're such a good writer. And they need people.

ME: All they have is articles about food drives. And student government.

SADIE: But it would be fun.

ME: Yeah.

SADIE: And you write all the time, anyway. I remember you were always writing something. Do you still do that? Get up in the middle of the night and start scribbling away?

ME: Sometimes.

SADIE: I'm telling you. They need people. Jill Kantor is always bugging me to do an article —

ME: So what happened with Will?

SADIE: Nothing. We broke up.

ME: That's what I heard.

SADIE: I know. It kind of dragged on in a way. So I had to say we were totally broken up. Officially.

ME: Officially.

SADIE: We still talk a little. Even though we're supposedly not going to.

ME: Huh.

SADIE: He says I'm too obsessed with my causes.

ME: You're not too obsessed with your causes. That's a stupid thing to say.

SADIE: Well, even if I am. That's me. You know?

ME: Yeah.

SADIE: What about you? Doesn't seem like you've gone out with anyone . . .

ME: No.

SADIE: Why not?

ME: Who would I go out with?

SADIE: I don't know. There must be somebody out there. I still don't understand why you didn't join the paper. Jill Kantor even asked me about you. You would totally like those guys. And it's so pointless not to contribute something.

ME: I did write this one thing I thought about sending in.

SADIE: Really, what is it?

ME: It's called "Destroy All Cars."

SADIE: "Destroy All Cars"? Is it a joke?

ME: No. Don't you think we should destroy all cars?

SADIE: *No.* How would we get to school?

ME: We'd have to figure something out. It would force us to rethink our concepts of transportation.

SADIE: But what about hybrid cars? Or cars that run on electricity?

ME: Where are we going to get enough electricity to keep all those soccer moms in minivans, driving to the mall to get their nails done?

SADIE: Through wind farms. Or solar power. And what do you have against soccer moms?

ME: Nothing. Except that I hate them.

SADIE: Your approach to these problems is not very logical.

The first time I saw Sadie, I was walking past a student activities table in the breezeway at our school. This was the beginning of sophomore year. Some students were trying to get people to come to the Annual Benefit Dance. If you brought two cans of food, you got in for free, and if you brought four cans, you got a raffle ticket to win an iPod Shuffle. They did it every year. It was kind of a joke, and nobody really went to the dance except for nerds and freshmen.

But that day, there were a lot of people gathered around the table. The whole breezeway was buzzing for some reason. I crowded forward to see what was up, and that's when I saw her. Sadie Kinnell. She was tall, with dark blue eyes and long black hair that swung slightly as she moved her head. She was in full Sadie mode: handing out flyers, buttons; explaining things; talking to four different people at once. She had so much energy. The crowd was mesmerized.

I didn't understand why someone like her would be wasting their time on a canned-food drive. It didn't seem right. I stood with the other people and listened to her talk about helping the needy. She really got into it. She sort of drilled her message right into you. When some people left, she turned to me and said, "I know the dance is sort of lame. But maybe we can make it better."

It was like she had read my mind.

I didn't know what to say back. I took one of the flyers. "But isn't a food drive sort of a band-aid solution?" I finally asked, over the murmur of the other people.

"What do you mean?" she said, handing buttons to some freshmen.

"So we give some cans of food to people," I said. "What does that solve?"

"It solves the problem of what they're going to eat that night," she said, her eyes locking on to mine.

I stared into her face. There was something about her that went right through me. She did something to my insides.

I quickly folded up the flyer and stuffed it in my pocket.

"Come to the dance," she said.

"I will," I said. I glanced at her one last time. Then I went to class.

All week I kept folding and unfolding that piece of paper. Then I went to the dance. I even wore my favorite shirt, which at that time was this dorky orange thing with a *Star Trek* collar. And the funny thing was, I went by myself, which no one does at our high school. Going to a dance by yourself is social suicide. But I did it anyway. I wasn't even worried. It was like some other person had taken over my body.

There weren't many people there. It was pretty much like it always was. Totally lame. But I didn't notice. I walked around. I looked for the girl in the breezeway, the girl who'd invited me.

When I didn't see her, I sat by myself at one of the tables. I didn't dance. Nobody did.

I finally decided she wasn't coming, so I stood up to go home. I was heading for the exit when a hand caught my elbow. I turned around and there she was: that bright face, those shining eyes. I was like, *whoa.*

She remembered me from the breezeway. She asked me my name. Then she asked me to dance. She said if we didn't get people dancing, they never would.

So we danced. And it was fun. Other people started to dance, too. And it got to be more fun.

Finally, she went off somewhere to help get the raffle together. I took a seat along the wall. In the darkness, I ran my hand through my hair. I tried not to think too much, I tried to stay calm, but deep down I knew something was happening to me. Something big.

Then a slow dance came on, one of the precious few. I immediately stood up and started looking around the gym for her. I tried to see back by the canned goods. I didn't want to be too obvious, but at the same time, I never wanted to find someone so badly in my life.

I saw her. She was heading my way, weaving through the crowd. She was looking for me. Just like I was looking for her.

We were both embarrassed, of course. And then when we got on the dance floor, we couldn't figure out how to put our arms around each other. But it was okay. We worked it out. Then we swayed back and forth and rotated and held each other like you do.

After the dance, Sadie waited for her mom to pick her up. I stood with her under the awning and watched the drizzle in the streetlight across the road. We talked more. I don't remember what about. It didn't matter. We were going to be together. We both knew it. What that meant exactly, I had no idea. I had never thought about having a girlfriend. I had no idea how that worked. I didn't understand anything in those days.

SADIE: That's so funny I ran into you. Like here we are, back at the library.

ME: Here we are.

SADIE: You should give me your cell number.

ME: I don't have a cell.

SADIE: Still? I just got one. My parents gave it to me on my birthday. I felt like the last person on earth to get one.

ME: Well, you're not. Since I don't have one.

SADIE: You should get one. They're so handy. Maybe you should ask for one for your birthday.

ME: I just had my birthday.

SADIE: Oh yeah. That's right. I noticed the day. I
thought about you. It's weird that I hardly ever
see you anymore.

ME: Yeah . . .

SADIE: Maybe we should . . . I don't know . . . hang
out some time.

Sadie's face was always the draw. That was the killer for
me. Her face. Because she's so smart. She doesn't always
act it, but she is. And she's reasonable. By that I don't
mean practical, I mean she understands the limits of
things, and the limits of people. She never has stupid
ideas. She never says she's going to do something that
you know she can't or won't do. You might think that's
not that unusual, but in high school, most girls still
think they're going to be the next American Idol. I'm
serious. They do not quite have a foothold on reality.
Sadie did. She was deeply intelligent, deeply real, even as
she tried to recycle plastic forks in the lunchroom. It's
hard to explain. It was in her eyes. It was in her
expression. It was even in the way she got annoyed with
you (me). She got stuff. You did not have to explain it
twice. She understood.

There was a protection thing, too. I thought she could
protect me. That sounds weird but that's what it felt like.
She's the kind of person that is constantly moving
forward. It's hard to hurt a person like that. And if you're
with them, you think you won't get hurt either.

SADIE: Here, give me your home number. Also, I want to see "Destroy All Cars." Is it a blog?

ME: No. I don't do blogs.

SADIE: Why not? Everyone else does.

ME: Exactly.

SADIE: How long is it?

ME: It's short.

SADIE: That reminds me. Did you hear about what's happening over by Carl Haney's house?

ME: No.

SADIE: Some developer is going to turn all those woods into a subdivision. Like where the pond is, on both sides of it.

ME: The pond? Are you serious?

SADIE: I know. Activist Club is going to do a petition. And I talked to a guy at *Willamette Week*. And I called the mayor's office and I'm meeting with their special zoning person. That's what I came down here for. To check the zoning records.

ME: How do you have time to do all this stuff?

SADIE: How do you have time to write in your journal all night?

ME: I don't. I just do it anyway.

SADIE: That's what I do.

PART
3

February 18

Rode around with Jessica Carlucci today after school. She had her mom's car. I stared out the window a lot. Jessica asked me why I was being so quiet and I told her about seeing Sadie at the library.

"I knew it," she said.

We drove to Pet World and I followed her around while she bought some vegetarian dog food for her dog. She told me about this college in New Mexico where you do nothing but read the classics of world literature. No *Intro to Basketweaving*. You start with Plato and work your way forward.

She's trying to get me interested in college. I don't know what I think about that. Of course my parents want me to go.

Later, I called Gabe and went to his house. We played ping-pong. Then we watched TV. I have not done any homework in three days.

Scary, the effect talking to Sadie for five minutes has on me. I have become useless, lethargic, unable to concentrate.

I don't want to start liking her again, that would be counterproductive.

Gabe counsels against it as well. "Get a new girlfriend," he tells me constantly. "Don't get caught in this all over again."

But what does he know? He still worships Renee, who barely acknowledges his existence.

James Hoff

Junior AP English

Mr. Cogsweiller

MAKEUP ASSIGNMENT: *personal reflection on a place or location*

A NIGHT AT THE MALL

I was at the mall, reading a book called *The Bell Jar,* when a goth girl started talking to me. She seemed to think I was goth, too, because of my black sweater and my long hair. Her name was Kristine. She had dyed black hair, red lipstick, and a ring in her eyebrow. She said that she had read the same book, and she liked it, and what was my name? I told her my name was Rob, though my actual name is James.

She sat down across from me. We talked about different things. Because Kristine was goth, she mostly had goth-style opinions. She was depressed, for starters. She liked weird, dark music you never heard of. And she hated authority of any kind. All of which were consistent with the goth philosophy.

After we talked for a while, she asked if I felt like going to a movie. I said okay and we went to see *The Hills Have Eyes 3,* which is about these mutants who got radiated by nuclear tests and murder people who happen to wander into the contaminated area. (Think about that for a second: There are now large sections of the earth where you can't go because they are so poisoned and radioactive that if you went there, you would die.)

Anyway, so then a Typical American Family gets lost in the contaminated area and that's when the fun begins. Mutants vs. Typical American Family. There was lots of gore and splattering blood. It was kind of hard to watch, actually. Kristine liked it. I kept glancing over at her as the movie played. She wasn't the most beautiful girl, but she was sort of appealing in her goth way. She had black nail polish on and bright red lipstick. I had never hung out with anyone who wore lipstick before.

So then after the movie, Kristine asked if I felt like driving around. I said okay, and we went to the parking lot and got her car. It was an old Pontiac sedan. It was kind of sad. Even though I hate cars, I still recognize the status implied by the different brands. That's another thing cars do for us. They put us in categories depending on what level of Consumer American we are. Poor people drive crap cars. You see a crap car, you know who's inside it.

Kristine wanted to get cigarettes. She was quitting smoking, or had been, but now, because of the scary movie, she was too riled up to not have a cigarette. So we drove to a not-so-great neighborhood, to a place called the Lucky Stop Market. We went there because Kristine knew the guy and he would sell her cigarettes.

It was pretty grim there at the Lucky Stop. I think someone was selling drugs by the restrooms. Kristine got her cigarettes, and then as she was paying, she turned to me and said, "Should I get some condoms?" I swear she said that. I hadn't thought about if we might need condoms. It was pretty much the furthest thing from my mind.

I shrugged. I didn't know. She bought them.

"Just in case," she said.

I got a Pepsi.

So now we were set. We had cigarettes and beverages and condoms. Also, back at the Lucky Stop, under the fluorescent lights, I had noticed that Kristine's forearms were covered with cut marks and burn scars. Not that there's anything wrong with that. I just mention it to paint a complete word picture.

We drove around. We ended up parked in a vacant lot by the river. She lit a cigarette and started talking about this guy named Dale who screwed her over. She met him at her job at Walgreens but he cheated on her with her best friend. Then he gave Kristine crabs when he cheated on the best friend with her. Then the best friend got arrested for throwing a rock through Dale's window and peeing in his car and trying to light his house on fire.

I drank my Pepsi.

At some point, Kristine decided that I wasn't her type. "You're like this nice boy from the suburbs," she said. She wasn't trying to be mean, that was her honest opinion. To prove her wrong, I leaned over and kissed her. She liked that. We started making out. She was a good kisser, slow and sexy, lots of lick-ing and touching of tongues. But she tasted like lipstick and cigarettes and I was worried I might get crabs. Eventually we stopped, and I slid back onto my side of the seat.

Driving back, I didn't want to tell her where I lived, so I told her to take me back to the mall, I could walk back from there. She dropped me off. Just before she pulled away, she said, "Nice to meet you, Rob." By then I'd forgotten I'd given her a fake name. For a second, I wasn't sure who she was talking to. But I recovered.

"Nice to meet you, too," I said.

The End

February 19

Mr. Cogweiller gave me an A– for my mall story paper and wrote on the bottom that I should submit it to the literary magazine as a short story. The problem is, it's not a story, it's true.

He also said I shouldn't mess up my writing with little asides. And that if I can, I should avoid constantly harping on my political agenda. That's so funny he thinks I have a political agenda. DUDE, IT'S NOT POLITICS, IT'S THE SURVIVAL OF OUR PLANET.

I think he's just saying that, though, to prove I'm not shocking him. Old Cogs, he may look like Mr. Oxford Button-Down, but deep down he still wants to be cool with the kids.

February 20

Sadie never called. Not that I thought she would.

I did email her "Destroy All Cars," though. She wrote back, "Thanks, James! I'll show it to the Activist Club."

Yeah, like they'll be able to deal with it.

I shouldn't be bitter. Sadie is just trying to be nice. She just wants to be friends again. Or at least make it so we can pass each other in the hall without electrical storm clouds forming.

I talked to Jessica about it. She seems to think it's a natural part of the healing process.

Gabe wants me to ask out one of Renee's friends so we can double-date.

The thing about asking out other girls is that they are other girls. They are not Sadie.

Other girls are CONSUMER AMERICANS. They are tedious and superficial and at some point they will want to know what my problem is.

And what will I say then?

February 21

There was an article in *The Oregonian* today about the
subdivision behind Carl Haney's house. It's true: They're
going to bulldoze the whole area. It's too bad because
the pond is a very popular spot among kids who live in
a certain area. People hang out there. And park there.
And party. It's like a tradition. Sadie and I even made out
there a couple times. I mean, it isn't a very *nice* pond, it
isn't like a public park. But that's part of what's cool
about it. It's an actual pond in an actual wilderness, with
weeds and mud and "critters" and whatnot. You have to
drive down this old dirt road to get to it. That's a pretty
rare thing in this area. Pretty much all the woods and
creeks and stuff have been developed. It was the last
place kids could hang out and actually be away
from civilization.

February 23

Went to the mall with Gabe and his mom this morning.
She had to buy some bath towels. Also, she can't resist
the makeup counters. Gabe wanted to look for some new
skateboard wheels. I went along for the ride.

We took the Ford Expedition, all of us spaced far
apart and strapped in so we could withstand impacts
from other Sports Utility Vehicles. If anything smaller
than an SUV crashed into us, well, that's too bad for
them. Those people should buy bigger cars if they want
to survive collisions. God knows *we* needed a big car —
we're buying bath towels.

We parked and went in and strolled through
Nordstrom. Gabe's mom got snagged by the first lab-
coated makeup person she saw. Gabe and I escaped the
evil makeup counters and found our way to Concourse B.

Concourse B is our favorite: the high ceilings, the
plastic plants, the steady flow of CONSUMER
AMERICANS moving like fish along an endless stream
of merchandise and consumables. Plus there's girls. That
was Gabe's main concern: where can we stand, sit, eat,
drink, and still have the widest range of girls to check
out. I was also somewhat interested in this.

We went to McDonald's first. Gabe's mom doesn't
like him to eat there because she thinks it's unhealthy.
But he does, anyway, on the sly. That's his little rebellion.
Unfortunately, the girl possibilities at McDonald's
were limited.

So we went to Deck, the skateboard store. That place is pretty cool, I have to admit. I wish I was better at skateboarding — they have the raddest stuff. Some seventh graders were skating around in the back, doing tricks on the carpet. Skateboarding is cool. Simple. Clean. Energy efficient.

Gabe finally bought his wheels and some stickers to go with them. After that we cruised down the concourse and came across something called Caribou Coffee, which we hadn't seen before. We were like, what's this? A new Starbucks rip-off? That uses the catchy name of an animal species we are no doubt wiping off the face of the earth? We were so there. Plus there was free coffee for the grand opening.

We went inside. We got some free coffees. We tried them. We stood around with the other Consumer Americans evaluating the new product. Some people liked the Caribou Coffee. Others, not so much. Is it too bitter? Too strong? What *is* a caribou anyway? Mall goers discussed it: "It's this thing like a horse." "Isn't it an island?" "It's like a dog, but it has fur that hangs down."

After we got bored at Caribou Coffee, we ventured onto Concourse B again to look for girls. Gabe wanted to stand outside Abercrombie & Fitch but I thought that was too obvious. So we sat on some benches instead. Gabe and I looking for girls has, historically, not been a big success. Even when we see ones we like, we're too afraid to talk to them. Even when we see ones who seem to like us, we're too afraid to move in their direction. And when we see girls who like us and actually come over and talk to us, we still screw it up (this has never actually happened, but if it did . . .). So the looking-for-girls thing is more like we're *observing* girls. And studying them. For future reference.

So we sat on the bench for a while and then a girl I actually recognized walked by, a girl who goes to our school. I elbowed Gabe to look, and he saw her, too. She seemed to be with her mom or some other adult. She glanced over and saw us, too.

For some reason, I waved to her. It was kind of a half-assed wave but I did it and she waved back, smiling a little, like: *Oh my God, I'm stuck with my mother, how much does this suck?*

A second later, she was gone. "Dude," I said to Gabe. "Who was that?"

"I don't know. But she waved to you."

"Lucy," I said, trying to think of her name. "It's Lucy something. She's a sophomore."

"Oh yeah, Lucy Branch," said Gabe. "Rich Herrington went to the Christmas dance with her last year."

"What's her deal?"

"Don't know. But she *totally* waved to you."

I tried to see if Lucy Branch was still in sight, but she had disappeared down Concourse B.

Lucy Branch, I thought. I liked the sound of it.

February 25

Lucy Branch does not have a definite look. Or rather she falls into that vague "Jeans and Urban Outfitters T-shirt" universe. She was wearing Nikes at the mall with a Ramones T-shirt. I doubt she even knows who the Ramones are. She looks more Classic Rock to me, but who knows? She does seem somewhat aggressive in her personality. Like she actually waved back to me at the mall. And today she did the same thing in the cafeteria, smiling and waving again. This caught me off guard and I spilled tartar sauce on myself.

She is signaling to me some form of romantic interest. I would not be brave enough to do that if I were her. Or maybe I would. I went to Sadie's stupid dance. Still, I don't know what to make of Lucy Branch. I can't tell if I would like her. I guess I would like any girl if I got physically close enough. Lucy is cute and she has a cute body. And she likes me. Or seems to. That is the important thing.

February 26

The fact that Lucy Branch might like me indicates to me that my look is not representing my true personality. She's not really my type at all. Can't she see that?

Or maybe girls don't care. It's like music, girls don't care what band it is, they just like the song.

Lucy is so different from Sadie. I can't tell what Lucy's into. Nothing, most likely. She's just a girl, just a person. She wakes up, goes to school, goes home, watches TV. I don't know who she's friends with. I feel sorry for her in some vague way but I don't know why.

But if she would have sex with me, what difference does it make what she's into?

Gabe had a thought: "Why do guys worry about what to say to girls? If they like you, whatever you say is going to work. And if they don't like you, nothing you say is going to make any difference."

That still leaves out the crucial part: How do they decide they like you?

February 27

Saw Lucy in the hall talking to a guy today. I was instantly jealous. Why do I like her so much? I don't even know her. I want her physically. That's really it. I've never wanted someone like that before. I ache when I see her.

With Sadie it was never about the physical. It was totally above that. But maybe that's what happens. You hit that late adolescent period and all thinking ends. You come right down to earth, right down to beast level. You become that thing girls talk about: a typical male being led around by his lower extremities.

It's hard to imagine talking to Lucy. But I can imagine sleeping with her. I have been imagining it quite regularly. I can't stop imagining it. Maybe it's time for my first Lucy Branch, my first truly physical relationship. And why do I assume it would be a bad thing? Maybe it's better with someone different from you. I could teach her how fluorocarbons affect the ozone. She could teach me about oral sex.

We would both become better people.

February 28

Saw Sadie after school today. She was talking with two of her Activist Club comrades.

Sadie sort of looked in my direction as I passed. She didn't say anything, though. Weird how I thought after our library conversation that something would happen. Nothing did.

Anyway, I am too busy contemplating the possibilities with Lucy Branch to think about anything else.

"Yes, Lucy, it is hot in this broken-down car in the middle of the desert, maybe we should take off our clothes. . . ."

"Of course you can stay in my tent here in the rain forest, Lucy. We'll just have to share my sleeping bag. . . ."

"I know it sucks that we're snowed in at this mountain cabin, Lucy, but at least there's two of us and lots of blankets. . . ."

And yet, no matter how much I obsess over Lucy Branch, Sadie remains, lurking in the back of my mind. My first girlfriend, my first love, my first everything. And the worst part: the impossibly high standard I'll measure everyone else against the rest of my life.

Thanks a lot, Sadie, for making every other girl seem like a brainless slug.

THE ROBOT SHOW

Jessica Carlucci and I went to the New Technologies Convention last night with her dad. There weren't as many robots as there have been in past years, though there were some dancing robots and some robots that fly and some nanobots that they put in your bloodstream that can tell if you have cancer or not.

There was other stuff, too. New cars, new games, new battery-operated clothing. There was a personal submarine with drink holders, which might come in handy in the future. Everything says "green" on it now, regardless of whether it actually is. That was kind of annoying.

The worst was a Chevy Avalanche they had right in the middle of the convention center. For those who don't know what a Chevy Avalanche is, it is a Deluxe Luxury Pickup Truck built in the shape of a penis. I think one could safely say it is one of the stupidest vehicles ever invented.

This particular Chevy Avalanche was painted green, and on the hood was a big sign that said THE NEW GENERATION OF ENVIRONMENTALLY FRIENDLY CARS. There were smaller signs on the different parts of it. On the wheels it said FRICTION RESISTANT FREE-ROLLING TIRES. On the gas cap: ABLE TO BURN GASOLINE AND ETHANOL. On the hood: NEW TECHNOLOGIES IMPROVE GAS MILEAGE 25%.

That was the one that killed me. *New technologies improve gas mileage 25%.* I couldn't get over that. Of course, being an MPG freak, I happen to know that the Chevy Avalanche gets an estimated 14 mpg, which means if you bought one and drove it around, it would actually get 10. Which means that a 25 percent increase would get it up to 12.5 miles per gallon. Which is . . . *ridiculous!*

I had a bit of a moment there, standing in front of the Chevy Avalanche. I've heard people say the government is corrupt or the oil companies are evil or whatever. I never listened. I never believed stuff like that. I figured somewhere, in some lab, there were scientists from the car companies seriously trying to improve gas mileage, or create cleaner emissions, or develop an electric car or a hybrid or whatever. But as I stood there, looking at this monstrosity and its signs about "free-rolling tires," I thought, *What if they aren't doing anything? What if they really don't care?*

I looked at the people standing around me. A dad was showing his kid the gleaming hubcaps on the "green" Chevy Avalanche. Other people were oohing and ahhhing over the "green" chrome exhaust pipes. And I thought: *Why would they bother doing anything, if people believe this crap?*

On the ride home, I told Jessica about the Chevy Avalanche. She thought it was funny that they were try-ing to pass off a luxury truck as "green." But she doesn't take any of this stuff as seriously as I do. She and her dad were laughing about the dancing robots. I ended up sitting in silence, lost in my own thoughts.

March 5

Gabe wants me to ask out Lucy Branch. He thinks I
need a girlfriend. He's been reminding me how popular
I was when I was with Sadie. People knew me and
talked to me. I did stuff and went places. Now, he says,
all I do is sulk and stay up too late and scribble in my
notebooks until midnight at Shari's. This is true, but
I reminded him that Karl Marx wrote his manifesto in
the library, surrounded by bums and weirdos. He
thinks that's great but that unless I want to become one
of those bums or weirdos, I need to hang out with some
actual people.

I'm thinking about it. The truth is, I have never asked
someone out on a Classic American Date. Sadie and I
never did that. We didn't have to. Also, I am not sure
Lucy is right for me. Unfortunately, I may not have any
other options. Because I have cut holes in my sweater
and have been seen reading books in the cafeteria, I have
declared myself to be some sort of fringe, radical,
intellectual type. Now I must face the consequences.

In the meantime, I walk around my neighborhood at
night and think about population. That is the key to all
our problems. People ask, "What can I do to help the
environment?" Answer: not exist. Nothing would be
better for the planet than us not being on it. We have
spread over the earth like a great rash, like an infestation

of killer insects. We annihilate every living thing in our path, devour resources, rip up the earth to get the oil and the gold and whatever other crap we think we need. We have shown no mercy to animals, plant life, forests, oceans. We have even destroyed segments of our own species, the ones too gentle to resist our most brutal impulses. We have ravaged the planet with our insane lust and greed, everywhere leaving behind horrendous pollution, toxic waste, and lethal contamination. We have shat in our own soup bowl. And now we are trying to eat around it.

Gabe is right. I don't look so good. I am pale and I have acne. That is common for people my age. I am an adolescent. I am becoming a "man." In some cultures, a seventeen-year-old is considered a man already. In our culture, I am considered a child. I do not feel like a child. I look at myself in the mirror and I want to lead a revolution. I want to tear my society down to the ground and start over. But maybe every seventeen-year-old thinks that.

One thing is for sure: People are not going to change. Our single worst problem is population growth, but adults are not capable of not having children. Adult CONSUMER AMERICANS are not capable of controlling any impulse they experience. Kids are cute. They must have them. The neighbors have kids. They must have them. Mrs. Jones is bored at the tennis club and she saw

another woman with a baby. She must have one. This is
how we operate. WE SEE SHINY OBJECTS — CARS,
PUPPIES, KITTENS, LITTLE BABIES — AND WE
MUST HAVE THEM. I think most adults figure
someone else will deal with the big problems. Someone
else will figure it out. And if they can't, well, we might
as well live it up for now. Nothing we can do. Might as
well get ours, while there's still something to get.

Sometimes I think about my relationship with Sadie. We
were like brother and sister, always bickering, but deeply
joined. I remember our fight about plastic fork recycling
in the lunchroom. We barely spoke to each other for a
week. But when we finally made up, it was like the
weight of the world was lifted off my shoulders.
    What would Lucy and I fight about? Or talk about? Or
do anything about? I am not the first boy to like a girl
based on her physical attributes. Lots of cute people go
out with other cute people based on mutual cuteness.
But how does that work? What holds them together?
Why do they care?
    Maybe they don't care.

It's true what Gabe said about Shari's Restaurant. I do
come here too much. I'm here right now. It's dark here,
warm, and there's lots of carpet. It's like being inside a
sponge. The waitresses bring me coffee the minute I sit
down. They know me here. They know my type: the
pimply kid writing poetry, or drawing wizards, or

writing *Star Trek* fan fiction. I hate being a kid. Are
any of these thoughts I have even logical? I have no idea.
At the same time, I look around at Shari's and I see the
people who hang out here. Truckers. Salesmen.
Divorcées. The common people. The people who punch
the clock. What do they think about? Anything? Can
they imagine real change? Can our government?
Can anybody?

Population. There are too many of us. But any time
people and animals come in contact, what is our first
response? SAVE THE PEOPLE. A bear wanders into a
neighborhood, lost and confused because there is no
more wilderness left for him to go to. What do the
authorities do? They shoot him. A coyote gets stuck in
someone's backyard? They shoot her. A wolf in
the town dump? The local deputies draw straws for the
privilege of shooting him. In any situation where a
human and a wild animal come together, and where
there is even the remotest possibility that the
human might be inconvenienced, the animal is
"destroyed." There are 300,000,000 people in the
United States. There are probably fewer than 300,000
bears. But the bear dies. The thinking is: We are
humans, we are precious, we are above the other
creatures. But there are too many of us already. We are
choking the world to death. Shouldn't we, logically, be
willing to sacrifice a few humans to save a bear? A bear
that we put in this situation in the first place?

Basically, the solution is that we have to stop having so many children and driving gas-guzzling tanks around. But we won't.

Gabe offered to get Lucy's number from her friend. I can't imagine calling her up. What would I say? I look terrible, anyway. I can barely talk. I walk around mumbling to myself, scratching my dirty hair, trying not to touch the zit on my neck.

And what would I do with her? Where would we go? I could take her to Shari's. "Welcome, Lucy. This is my home, these are my people."

God help me.

March 6

Junior Hall. End of lunch period.

ME: Hey, Lucy.
LUCY (*at her locker*): Oh . . . James . . .
ME: Hey.
LUCY: Hey.
ME: What's up?
LUCY: Not much. Getting ready for class.
ME: Oh yeah?
LUCY: Yeah. What's up with you?
ME: Nothing. I just . . . I just saw you and thought I
     should, you know . . . see what's up.
LUCY: Not much. You're lookin' at it!
ME: Yeah. I guess so.
LUCY: Yeah.
ME: . . .
LUCY: . . .
ME: So I, uh . . . saw you at the mall the other day.
LUCY: I saw you, too.
ME: Concourse B.
LUCY: What?
ME: That's where you were. On Concourse B.
LUCY: Oh.
ME: Because the different sections have different
     names? Like Concourse A? And Concourse B?
LUCY: Oh.
ME: Sometimes I notice things like that.

LUCY: I just try to remember where I parked! Ha ha.

ME: Me, too. I hate that. Ha ha —

LUCY: Ha ha. Or at Nordstrom, you go out the wrong door and then you're in this, like, sea of cars.

ME: Ha ha. I hate cars.

LUCY: And they have those letters you can never remember.

ME: I know. It's not very linear.

LUCY: It can get confusing. Ha ha.

ME: Yeah, I know what you mean —

LUCY: Ha ha.

ME: Ha ha.

LUCY: . . .

ME: So, yeah. I guess the reason I wanted to . . .

LUCY: Yeah?

ME: Stop by, and, you know, say hi . . . and see what was up . . . is . . .

LUCY: Is?

ME: That's the thing . . . I wanted to . . . ask you. Do you ever, like . . .

LUCY: What?

ME: Do you ever . . . or would you ever, like, wanna . . . you know . . . go to a movie or something . . . ?

LUCY: Oh.

ME: —

LUCY: —

ME: I mean, not like, not —

LUCY: No. That's okay. What movie?

ME: Just whatever. A movie.

LUCY: Movies are good.

ME: We could just, you know . . . or we don't
have to —

LUCY: No, but yeah, if you want to . . . we could.

ME: Which one, though? Or do you care?

LUCY: I don't care. I just. I kinda don't like scary
movies.

ME: Yeah? Me neither.

LUCY: My cousin rented *The Hills Have Eyes 3*. Oh
my God. Have you seen that?

ME: Kinda, yeah —

LUCY: Oh my God, it was so gross. I mean, like,
this guy gets dropped in a well, with all these
human heads bobbing around! —

ME: I hate bobbing heads.

LUCY: Yeah, right? Ha ha. It was disgusting.

ME: Okay. Well. Like maybe some other one then?

LUCY: I would be into that.

ME: When? Like, when would be a good time?

LUCY: When were you thinking?

ME: This weekend, possibly? If you can.
Because . . . or you know . . . if you're not busy.

LUCY: No, I can. But not on Saturday. Because I
have to babysit.

ME: We could meet at the theater.

LUCY: Okay, or. Do you have a car?

ME: Not at the moment.

LUCY: Okay. We could meet there.

ME: So is Friday okay?

LUCY: Friday works.

ME: Yeah. Friday. Maybe I should email you.

LUCY: Email?

ME: Or call you. I'll call you. I'll totally call you.

LUCY: Yeah, okay. Why don't you call me?

ME: I'll call you. What movie, though?

LUCY: I don't know. I don't know what you like.

ME: I'll call you.

LUCY: You can pick. Do you have my number?

ME: No. Can you give it to me?

LUCY: Here. Wait. I'll write it down.

ME: Cool. Thanks. I'll call you.

PORTRAIT OF A YOUNG MAN
ON A DATE (A SHORT STORY)

The boy sits on his bed and thinks. He has never been on a real date before. He is extremely nervous. He feels physically ill. He tries to remember why he wanted to do this. He can't remember.

He puts on his coat and leaves his house and rides the bus downtown to the movie theater. He has left plenty of time to get there, but the bus ride takes forever. He can't believe how long it takes. The bus stops every two seconds to let on some weird person who can't speak English or doesn't understand money or needs directions to some other town or city or country. Then a very large woman gets on with eight shopping bags but she doesn't have enough money so the driver kicks her off and she has to move her very large self and all her eight bags back off the bus, which takes about an hour.

The boy is totally freaking out.

He gets downtown and walks into the movie theater and his heart is racing and he feels like he's going to puke. He buys two tickets and sits in the lobby and waits for his date.

He stares out the glass doors of the theater and he doesn't know what he's doing. He wants to run away. He looks at the tickets. The movie they're seeing, the movie he chose, is in French. HE HAS NO IDEA WHY HE CHOSE A FRENCH MOVIE. THAT WAS EXTREMELY

STUPID. So he sits there, gripping the two tickets in his sweaty hands, waiting for his date.

The girl arrives. His date. She comes in and she's wearing jeans and Pro-Keds and a Ramones T-shirt under her coat. She might even have a little eye makeup on, though the boy is too nervous to look at her face.

She goes to the counter where they sell the tickets but the boy tells her he already got her ticket and he jams it in her face in a clumsy, graceless movement.

She takes the ticket. She looks around the old theater. It's called Cinema 21. It's known for playing strange, artsy movies, including movies in French. The boy thought it would impress her. Plus there was an article in the newspaper saying the French movie was good. But now the boy realizes that the movie reviewer is probably just a snob, trying to impress his readers by liking French movies. Just like he is trying to impress his date. He sees that all of human existence is people trying to impress other people. He wishes he was at home or at his favorite 24-hour restaurant writing this, instead of actually doing it.

His date wants to pay him back for the ticket but he won't let her, so then she wants to buy the popcorn. He waits while she buys it and they go to their seats. They eat popcorn. That's when he tells her the movie is in French. She says, "How are we going to understand it?" He says there are subtitles, like on a DVD.

"Oh," she says.

The movie sucks. It's totally boring and it's two hours and fifteen minutes long. The boy is too freaked out to suggest they leave. So he sits there. So does she, chomping her popcorn until it's gone. The movie is about a man whose daughter runs away, so he drives around Paris and argues with his wife in French. The car he drives is one of those miniature French ones that probably get 100 mpg. Those would be good to have in America, but nobody would buy them, because you can't impress people with a little car. You have to have a big stupid ridiculous car in America or people think you're a wuss.

After the movie, the boy and the girl leave the theater and walk around. The girl's big sister is home from college and they're going to call her when they're done hanging out. They go to a café near the theater. Again, the boy hopes to impress his date with his knowledge of interesting cafés downtown. She doesn't notice. They order two hot chocolates.

The girl has long brown hair, brown eyes, a pretty face, a cute body. When he asked her out, the boy figured they'd go to the movie, walk around, make out a little. They would do this a couple more times, they would get to know each other, come to like each other, and eventually they would have sex. She already likes him, after all. And she agreed to go to the movie. He thinks this is pretty much a sure thing; he just has to put the time in.

But he is wrong. This is the opposite of a sure thing. This is fingernails on a blackboard. Especially sitting in the café. It is just about the worst hour he has ever spent in his life. Trying to talk to her, trying to act natural, trying to drink the hot chocolate. Nothing is easy. Everything is impossible. He spills his hot chocolate. It's like he's forgotten how to use a cup.

The girl calls her sister and she comes and picks them up. The boy sits with the girl in the backseat. The minute they get in the car, the girl and her older sister start talking about family matters. They chatter away about this and that. It makes the boy feel bad. The conversation was so stilted at the café. And now finally his date can talk freely. She is finally able to relax.

He gives directions to his house. There seems to be no chance for a good-night kiss as they pull up. He says good-bye and gets out. The girl looks a little disappointed as he shuts the door. Then she calls for him to wait. She gets out and comes around and kisses him. It's just a peck but it's on the lips. Then she runs around to her side of the car and gets back in.

The boy goes inside with the knowledge that he is a total idiot.

The End

PART
4

A HOFF FAMILY VACATION

After preparing myself for a typical nothing-happening Spring Break, there has been a change of plans.

The Hoff family is going on vacation.

My dad has decided to take us to Sun River. It's a last minute decision, which is always the case with my dad doing something nice for the family. One day we're sitting around twiddling our thumbs, the next day we're frantically packing the Honda Pilot at five in the morning. The sudden change of plans obviously has to do with Dad wanting to meet someone or impress the other executives at his work. He would not do this otherwise.

In case anyone cares, my dad works for a company that makes artificial parts for your body, like plastic kneecaps, or titanium hip joints, or even whole arms or legs if you lose yours in one of our glorious wars against non-consumers. He doesn't actually do anything there, he just talks on the phone. He has a big, commanding phone voice. I hear it at home sometimes. He makes the big bucks sounding like he's better than other people, pretending he knows what he's talking about. My dad's kind of a scumbag, did I mention that? But that's okay. The main way to rise up in your average American Corporation is to be a total scumbag.

So we get to Sun River and we pull in through the heavily guarded gate and the whole place turns out to be

one big playground for Luxury SUVs. EVERY SINGLE
VEHICLE WITHIN THE WALLED PREMISES OF THE
SUN RIVER RESORT IS A SNORTING, PIGLIKE, GAS-
GUZZLING TRAVESTY OF MOTOR TRANSPORT.

My sister, Libby, who's been watching *Gilmore Girls*
on her portable DVD player, puts it away, so she can
watch the cute boys throwing snowballs in one of the
parking lots. There are cute girls, too, in down vests and
bouncy winter hats. They jump in and out of Cadillac
Escalades and Range Rovers, laughing, their white teeth
shining, throwing one last snowball before they slam the
door of their parents' $80,000 vehicles.

This is probably what college looks like.

We proceed to our rented cabin, where we unpack
and settle in. Later, my sister and I walk to the main
lodge where there's a place called the TeenZone, according to my mom's brochure. This turns out to be an
arcade/burger-joint kind of place. I order some fries and
sit in a booth and read a book called *Black Elk Speaks*,
which Mr. Cogweiller recommended. Libby walks
around and plays video games, checking out the other
people as she does. She has more social possibilities in
a place like this than I do. She's a prep, what can I say?
She has cute, normal friends. She likes cute, normal
boys. She's not going to think about the destruction of
the world until the last possible second, when all the
other cute, normal people think about it.

Black Elk Speaks is about the Lakota Indians of the
central plains. Black Elk himself was a little kid when the

first white people showed up, so his story pretty much covers the gradual disintegration of his tribe, thanks to the "gnawing flood" of the white men. The Lakota are cheated, herded, imprisoned, and eventually massacred by the white people. Also, Black Elk gets to watch us kill just about every living buffalo in North America. We do this by shooting them from trains. For sport.

A little bell rings, which means my fries are ready. I pay for them and sit and eat a couple. Libby comes and eats some, too. She's found a girl she knows. The two of them sit across from me, eating fries and chattering about schools and people they might know in common.

I get bored and decide to walk around. I go upstairs and stand in the main lobby and watch a limousine pull up, gleaming in the cold desert air. There are people in suits standing around, men in "dress" black cowboy boots, women with Botoxed faces. Maybe these are the people my dad came here to network with.

I think about my mom back at the cabin with my dad. I'm not a huge fan of my dad — I guess that's pretty obvious. He has a way about him, though. He is good at making people do stuff. Forcing you. Manipulating you. People like him rule the world. Maybe I should be glad. Our family has everything *we* need.

I look up at the ceiling of the big main room. It's designed to look like a Native American lodge, with huge wooden beams, all of them going into the center like spokes on a wheel.

I miss my mom. I mean, it's not like she went somewhere. She's right downstairs every morning when I wake up. But not really. Not totally.

I walk around more. There are nice carpeted halls on the second floor, leather couches, old photographs of ranches and early settlements. I find two high school girls talking on cell phones. They wear sweatshirts, sweatpants; their hair is pulled back in neat ponytails. They look at their nails while they talk. Boyfriends back home, no doubt. I pass them and go outside, onto the deck. The stars are out. And you can see Mount Bachelor standing in the distance. Silent, god-like, Mount Bachelor. What if, when the polar ice caps melt, the oceans rise so high that the mountains are the only land that's left on earth? That would be weird. Like only the stuff on those mountains would still be alive, like alpine flowers or certain birds. Gabe says birds can survive anything. They've been here longer than any other species. That would be funny if, in the future, aliens came to earth and found this water world, with only a couple tiny islands sticking up, and they moved here and set up floating colonies and lived here for hundreds of years, and then one day a couple aliens decided to explore the ocean and went down there and discovered our abandoned cities. *Wow,* they'd say in their alien language, *someone was here before!* All the other aliens would get very excited. There would be TV specials about us. They would have pictures of what they think we looked like. But then the buzz would die down. The average alien wouldn't care that much. Eventually it would only be the geeky scientist aliens who would think about it. Nobody else would really care. They'd have their own problems.

It's cold on the deck so I go back downstairs to the TeenZone. Libby wants to stay and hang out with her new friend. So I slip *Black Elk Speaks* into my coat pocket and walk home to the cabin without her, which turns out to be a mistake.

ME (*walking in*): Hey.
MOM: How was the lodge?
ME: Okay.
DAD: Where's your sister?
ME: She met some girl she knew.
MOM: What? You left Libby?
ME: I didn't leave her. She met some girl she knew.
DAD: Where is she now?
ME: I don't know. Back at the teen place.
MOM: You can't just leave your sister!
ME: She's thirteen. She's fine.
MOM: It's too late for her.
ME: It's not even ten o'clock.
DAD: She can't walk home by herself.
ME: She met some people. And why can't she walk home? There's nobody here but rich people.
DAD: Don't start giving us attitude. This is Libby we're talking about.
ME: What attitude?
MOM (*to Dad*): Do you think she's okay?

DAD (*to Mom*): I'll drive over there.

MOM (*to Dad*): Where do you think she is?

DAD (*to Mom*): I don't know. I'll find her.

ME: She's at the stupid TeenZone place. In the basement of the lodge.

MOM: How long ago was that?

ME: Ten minutes?

DAD: This is not responsible behavior, James. You do not leave your sister. You do not leave family members alone in strange places.

ME: You left us.

DAD: What?

MOM: What did you just say?

DAD: Answer me, James. What did you just say to me?

MOM: Answer him, James. What did you say?

ME: I said, *You left us.*

MOM: Are you trying to ruin this trip? Are you trying to ruin this entire vacation?

ME: No.

DAD: Well, that's what you're doing.

Issues (A Personal Essay)

When my dad left our family, I went to this guy in a sweater vest for counseling. He was a doctor of some sort. My parents paid him. Normally, I would not agree to this. I generally avoid people in sweater vests but this was a difficult time, and people wanted me to do it, so I did.

Going to counseling was another example of CON-SUMER AMERICANS solving problems by buying stuff. Our solution to all problems is to buy something. Buying me time with this guy was a waste of money, but it made everyone feel better. Almost everything we buy IS A WASTE OF MONEY but it usually succeeds in MAKING US FEEL BETTER.

Which is not to say I wasn't upset at that time – I was – but it was not a particularly mysterious feeling. It was the usual *holy crap, my parents are splitting up* feeling. You probably don't need years of mental health training to understand it. But I went to the guy anyway and we talked and we "sorted things out." The main things we sorted out were that my dad is self-centered, my mom is emotionally distant, and I have "anger issues."

I was mostly angry at my dad. My counselor said this was partly because my dad and I were so much alike. Whenever he pointed this out, he acted very proud of himself, like this was a profound insight. I did not think this was a profound insight. *Of course* people are like their parents; it's called *genetics.*

During the separation, Libby and I were living with my mom, so we mostly heard her side of things. But to be brutally honest, I could see my dad's side, too. He got sick of us. It happens. You get sick of people. I know parents aren't supposed to do that, but I could see how they could. Dad got bored and annoyed and pissed off and he bailed. Then he saw how lame being a fifty-year-old divorced loser was going to be and he came back. My sister, Libby, totally freaked. She didn't understand it at all. But I did. It still made me mad but it was not incomprehensible.

My counselor's office was across the street from our local mall. Sometimes I walked over to the mall afterward and got a smoothie or whatever and thought about what we had discussed. I suppose I did learn a few things from my time with the counselor. I just can't remember what they are.

The main thing about when your parents split up is that they stop being your parents. They become like couples you know at your school who are breaking up. The whole WE ARE YOUR ALL-KNOWING AND ALL-POWERFUL PARENTAL FIGURES breaks down and they become Kayla and Josh having a fight in the parking lot. That's the part that screws up the kids. The feeling that there are suddenly no ALL-POWERFUL PARENTAL FIGURES standing over them anymore. Kids need that. They need the protection. It's sort of sad how fragile we are, how dependent. The whole situation is just embarrassing, when you get right down to it. Which is why it would be better if it didn't happen.

But it did, so there you go. And then my dad came back and there were all sorts of weird mornings and weird evenings and weird this and that. "Things change," my mother used to say to us, during the worst of it. They sure do.

A HOFF FAMILY VACATION (continued)

The "leaving your sister at the TeenZone" controversy blows over and the next day we pack up our snowboards and go to Mount Bachelor. Riding on the chair lift, I think about sophomore-year Christmas, when we went to Costa Rica on a different last-second vacation. Sadie and I had been going out for about three months at that time and it was weird because I didn't know what I was supposed to do when we were apart. I called her a couple times, but my parents didn't want to pay the international rates. So then I wrote her a letter. Like on paper, with a pen, and sent it through the mail. Sadie loved that. She never shut up about "the letter." It was two pages, in my bad hand-writing. It was pretty sappy, actually. It said things like *I will love you for as long as the trees whisper in the moonlight, for as long as the mountains stand guard over the sea.* Or some crap like that. I kid you not. I wrote that. I should give myself more credit. I was an okay boyfriend.

That night we go back to the TeenZone and meet up with Libby's friend, Tasha. It turns out she lives nearby and they know each other from horse camp. Tasha's all right. She's an eighth grader like Libby, but she's more mature somehow. The three of us play video games and goof around in the lodge. Tasha kind of flirts with me. That's a little weird. Also, she does that thing where she sort of challenges you, calling you on stuff. But I don't mind. She's funny. And it's not like there's anyone else to talk to.

It snows all night on Wednesday, and Thursday is a spectacular day on the mountain. Libby and I ride up on the ski bus and I stare out the window at the mountain stream, semi-frozen, beside the road. I imagine myself as a young Lakota brave, picking my way along the creek bed on horseback. The warm sun, the blue sky, the muffled silence of the snowy forest — how permanent the natural world would seem to that person. And how wrong he would be.

Later, after dinner, Libby and I walk back to the TeenZone. Libby catches a stray snowflake in her mouth on the road. She says to me, "See, the world is not in such bad shape." Tasha is waiting for us and gets even more flirty when she sees me. She and I talk a lot that night. We keep ending up alone in odd places and having strange little conversations.

TASHA: So how far have you gone?
ME: What do you mean?
TASHA: You know.
ME: Not that far.
TASIIA: But you're in high school! And you had a
      girlfriend!
ME: Just because you're in high school doesn't
      mean *that* happens.
TASHA: That's not what I heard.
ME: Well, you heard wrong.

Or:

TASHA: Do you think there's a difference between being in love and being in lust?

ME: I hope so.

TASHA: What's the difference?

ME: Being in lust is just horniness.

TASHA: But it's not, though. When you're in lust, it's still about that one person. It's like love but with your body.

ME: Yeah, like you know so much about it.

TASHA: I know a lot about it. More than you, from the sounds of it.

Or:

TASHA: Did you ever get so passionate with your girlfriend you couldn't control yourself?

ME: I can always control myself.

TASHA: Is that really passion, though? Isn't passion when you totally lose yourself in the other person?

ME: On TV maybe. I don't live on TV.

TASHA: If I'm not *intoxicated* by a person, I won't waste my time. Why should I?

ME: That's the kind of thing people say on TV.

Later, when it's time to go home, Tasha and I end up standing together on the steps in front of the lodge. We're waiting for my sister, who's inside looking for her coat. We stand for a moment surrounded by the snow and the trees and the glowing moon. Suddenly, Tasha turns to me and gives me this dramatic look. It's like she thinks we're wildly in love and the whole night has been building up to this moment and now I'm supposed to take her into my arms and kiss her passionately.

I'm like, dude, you're *fourteen.*

So we just stand there until my sister comes out.

Later, I feel bad. I do like Tasha. She's fun to argue with. People are interesting sometimes. I forget that. They're interesting and complicated and sorta cute sometimes.

On Friday night, my dad wants to have a family activity. So we go ice-skating. It's me and my mom and my dad and my sister. It's like we're all together. It's like a beautiful dream. It's like the Disney Channel. Except that my dad and I hate each other. And my mom hates herself. And my sister is humiliated by the bunch of us. And I'm secretly waiting for the inevitable devastation of our entire civilization.

But except for that.

On our last night, there's an 80s Dance Party at the TeenZone. I go with Libby. I've never done so many social things with Libby, so it's been an interesting week in terms of that. We really are "being a family," whatever that means. We arrange to meet Tasha. I'm looking forward to that, actually. Could I be falling for her? No. She's just entertaining.

But then Tasha shows up and she's dressed up all

sexy. I don't know what to make of that. I mean, she's got eye shadow and lip gloss and this low-cut dress on, like she's trying to show cleavage. But she doesn't have anything to show.

The music starts. "Girls on Film" is the first song. Tasha seems very focused on me. We dance a little. Then Libby goes off somewhere and leaves us alone, which is not good. Tasha and I end up dancing close and she gets a little touchy. So then I suggest we play video games, to hopefully keep things under control, but that's just as bad. She's bumping shoulders, bumping hips, I feel her hand graze my butt at one point. The hard part is, she smells good. And the top of her head seems to fit perfectly right under my chin. And there's only so many times a girl can touch you and lean against you and brush her fingertips across your arm before you start to respond. . . .

So we kiss. It just sort of happens, just for a second, next to Intergalactic Commandos or whatever. Then, before I can say anything, she's pulled me into this little storage room. We really start making out then. It's pretty crazy. After a minute of this, she looks up at me with one of her dramatic expressions.

"There's something I haven't told you," she says. "I have a boyfriend."

"Good!" I say back.

That makes her mad. We go back to the dance and I try to act normal, but she keeps giving me these angry looks. It's all very awkward. Especially when Libby comes back. The two of them go off and talk, and they both ignore me after that.

We drive home on Sunday. Libby and I sit in the back of the Pilot. We wear our seat belts and don't look at each other. She's probably not thrilled about the whole Tasha situation. It was pretty weird.

We leave Sun River and get back on the main highway. Instantly, the outside world changes from shiny SUVs, shiny people, shiny eighth grade girls to dirty trucks, broken-down cars, dull-faced people looking across at you. I think about Tasha, how she rested her hand on the small of my back during the video games. How she raised her face so slyly up toward mine for that first kiss. At one point she whispered, *"I like how you touch me."* Or some crazy thing. She's in eighth grade!! Unbelievable.

Meanwhile, in the front seat, my dad is cursing the lack of radio reception. My mom is checking our home messages with her cell. There's a message for me, she says. That's a surprise. She hands me the cell phone and tells me to push 1.

I push it and listen: *"Hey, James, Sadie here. I want to talk to you about something. If you wouldn't mind. You're probably off somewhere on vacation but can you give me a call when you get this? Thanks. See you."* I lower the phone from my ear.

Wow, I think.

Wow.

James Hoff

Junior AP English

Mr. Cogweiller

EXTRA CREDIT ASSIGNMENT: *four-page paper on topic of your choice*

POSSIBILITIES OF HOPE

Many people come up to me – well, no one has actually, but theoretically if someone came up to me – and asked, "James, what can I do to help stop the destruction of the planet and everything on it?" To these individuals I would say, "Fear not. There is hope."

I can't believe Sadie called me.

First of all, consider Native Americans. They are a model of sustainability. They lived with nature. Not on top of it. Not beating it with a baseball bat. They integrated themselves into the natural order of things, and did so with respect for other species and humility toward the earth.

I wonder what Sadie wants. Don't think about it. She called. So call her back.

Other native cultures – the tribes of New Guinea, for instance – managed to thrive without any technological advancement. Did they somehow sense the suicidal nature of continuous development? Oddly enough, we think of these peoples' lack of ambition as a sign of their inferior culture. They aren't "driven."

They don't "work hard/play hard" like we do. But the truth is, they are happy and healthy. They have established a harmonious existence on the earth.

I should have gotten some sun. And I have a new zit starting on my nose, which I can feel. I've gotta stop touching it.

Other cultures – the Greeks, for instance – were able to downshift from their dominant place as a center of trade and commerce. They were able to stop growing, stop conquering, and simply exist, content within themselves, not suffering from low self-esteem.

What could she want to talk about? What if it's something about Will? What if she wants to meet somewhere, to talk, and I end up alone with her. I'll kiss her. I totally will. No, I won't. That would totally freak her out.

In other places, like Oslo, there is a sense of planning. There is an overriding intelligence to everything people do. People in Oslo would *never* buy a vehicle that gets ten miles to the gallon. It doesn't make *sense.* Oslonians don't allow lumber companies to destroy their forests. Or car companies to sit on their asses and not develop more efficient vehicles. They *think* about the consequences of things before they do them. Our government is mainly concerned with keeping us buying stuff, the crappier the better. But our government is also somewhat fluid. Which means there *is* a chance for change.

The End
[Not handed in]

A HOFF FAMILY VACATION (continued)

When we get home from Sun River, I bolt for the house and run straight for the phone. But then my dad yells at me and says I have to help unpack, so I run back out and empty the crap out of the car and drop it on Libby, who refuses to catch it. Most of it crashes on the pavement, and a few things roll down the driveway. Libby stands there with her arms crossed. She says, "Why don't you go call Sadie instead of trashing our stuff?"

She knows Sadie called because my stupid mom announced it to the car after I listened to the message. My mom was like: "So are you and Sadie friends now?" No, Mom. We're not friends. But we're still in love with each other and we never had sex. Not to mention that she believes in positivity and the goodness of the human spirit while I believe in nothingness and the conflicted nature of the soul. So the "getting back together" thing isn't going so great. But I'm trying.

Anyway, so I pick up the crap off the driveway and run inside, but now it's like 10:15 at night and I'm not sure I should call this late. On the other hand, if I don't call her, there's the danger that I'll see her at school and she might come up to me in the crowded hallway and say whatever she wants to say and then I won't get a chance to talk to her privately. So I bound up the stairs and call Gabe really quick to see what he thinks, but he doesn't answer. Then I call Jessica, who is perplexed by the problem.

"What do you think she wants?" she asks.

"I have no idea," I answer.

So the "getting advice at the last minute" thing doesn't go anywhere. Which means it's up to me. I go to my room and flop on my bed and lie there for a second. I stare out the window at the trees outside. I still remember her home number by heart. I dial it and lie there. I put the phone to my ear. It rings. It answers.

"Hello?" says Sadie Kinnell.

It's the most natural thing in the world to talk to her. Even though the rest of me is shivering with nerves, my voice sounds calm and clear, totally normal, my best self, which she always seemed to bring out.

She asks about my vacation, where we went, how it was. I tell her, going heavy on the mountains and the snowboarding and leaving out the fourteen-year-old drama queen. I ask if she's ever read *Black Elk Speaks*. She has, of course. She says it broke her heart.

"Me, too," I say back.

I continue along, conversing, asking questions. It is so great to talk to her, to actually discuss things, to not have to edit myself or pretend in any way. *Oh my god,* I think, I AM STILL SO TOTALLY IN LOVE WITH HER. I want to cry. But I don't. I keep my mouth shut and listen and she conveniently starts talking about the pond by Carl Haney's house and how they're draining all the swamp area nearby, which will destroy the habitats of the local ducks and frogs and stuff. "That sucks," I repeat several times. She says she talked to a woman who runs an organization that's trying to stop the development. It's called Save the Wetlands, and they're getting a petition going to get the zoning board to approach the city council, etc. etc. I don't really follow this part. The point is, this woman needs people to get signatures. Sadie is going to do it. Would I be interested? It would only be a couple days a week, after school. . . .

I say yes. Of course I do. I say yes before she's even finished telling me what exactly we're doing. Yes yes yes. I will do it. Yes.

PART
5

James Hoff
Junior AP English
Mr. Cogweiller
EXTRA CREDIT ASSIGNMENT: *four-page paper on topic of your choice*

THE LESSONS OF OSLO

I went to Oslo with my dad when I was in seventh grade. He was going to a meeting there for work and he took me. We landed at the airport and went in a taxi to a big hotel in the city. At first, Oslo looked like any other city. But then I began to notice how organized it was. Like the lines on the road, the way the traffic lights worked, there was an advanced logic to things.

We went to the hotel and had lunch. My dad said the food in Oslo wasn't so great, but I liked it. There were lots of rolls. The cups and bowls were different. The plates were square. The forks were stubbier than American forks.

That afternoon, my dad went to a meeting and I stayed in the hotel. He said I could walk around if I wanted, but I was afraid, so I stayed in the room and read my Harry Potter book. After a while, though, I stopped reading and looked out the window. It was cold and misty and very gray outside. The cars were smaller than our cars. And the trucks seemed like toys some-how. I thought, *These poor people. They can't afford real trucks. They have to do everything really small and puny because they're not Americans like us.*

I went downstairs. I told the lady at the front desk that I was going for a walk. I stepped through the sliding glass doors and onto the street. It was very cold, but people were walking around. The Oslonians looked different from Americans. The actual shape of their faces was different. But they were very trim and well dressed. I was careful to stay out of their way. They looked busy.

I walked down the main street. Everyone had the latest cell phones and headsets. They had their odd minicars, and their Mercedes buses and their sleek, colorful streetcars. I went into a supermarket and everything was small and compact and computerized. It was like being in a science fiction movie, but only ten years in the future. Everything felt like it was designed very carefully. Everything was there for a reason. And it wasn't like they were walking around congratulating themselves about it. They just did it because that was the logical thing to do.

There were no strip malls in Oslo. There was no litter. There was a McDonald's, though, and I went there and the French fries tasted funny. I mean, it wasn't a perfect place. But it was different. That was the lesson. Things can be different. You don't have to keep doing things the exact same way. You can change. A lot of people do things differently and so can we.

The End

March 19

A– from Cogweiller. Barely made a mark on it. Wrote: *Interesting, good description of physical location* on the bottom.

March 20

At school today, Sadie came to my locker and gave me my clipboard and the petition sheets for Save the Wetlands. She told me that my days will be Tuesday and Thursday. Then she explained how you approach people and what you're supposed to say.

She had it all on a printout. While she showed me, she breathed on me and stood really close. Our forearms touched. She pointed out my location on the map: right in front of Powell's Bookstore downtown. She said it would be fun. She said I'd meet interesting people.

I was like, "Wait. Aren't you going to be there?"

She said no, her days are Monday and Wednesday. And she was at a different location, out by the airport.

I was like, "I thought we were doing this together?"

She said we were, but only in different places. And on different days.

So then I couldn't say anything more because that would be too embarrassing and would show that I don't really care so much about saving the ducks or the frogs or whatever. I mean, I do, but not enough to go stand on a street corner by myself, harassing people to sign a piece of paper — which won't really help anything anyway, not in the long run.

So I just grumbled and acted annoyed like I used to when we were going out and Sadie wanted me to do some weird thing I didn't want to do, but that, usually, I was glad I did, after I did it.

March 23

Had a talk with Mom last night. She asked me about
college stuff. Had I been looking into it? Did I have any
thoughts?

I knew that was coming. Of course my dad will want
me to apply to Harvard or some god-awful place so he
can brag to his friends.

I can't imagine where I would go. When I look
around at the seniors who are going to top colleges, they
seem like the biggest suck-ups imaginable. And the state
colleges seem like continuous frat parties. I guess I
could go to some freaky alternative college and grow my
own hemp or whatever.

March 24

Another college conversation with Mom this morning.

"There's another thing about the college situation," she said, as she poured coffee.

"What's that?"

"Your dad wants to buy you a car."

That was a bit of a shock.

"I think his idea is," said my mother calmly, "if you went to college here on the West Coast, you know, you'd be able to come home. . . ."

A car, I thought. *My own car. To feed and pet and clean up after . . .*

"I sorta hate cars, though," I said.

"I know. I tried to tell him that. He can't believe that anyone your age wouldn't want one. I think he's hoping a car would be that little nudge to get you interested in going to college."

"So if I take the car, I gotta go to college."

"Something like that."

"Has Dad ever met me?"

"He's just remembering his own college days. That's all it is. He's just trying to help."

James Hoff
Junior AP English
Mr. Cogweiller
ASSIGNMENT: *four-page paper on an activity you have participated in outside of school*

A PARTIAL LIST AND DESCRIPTION OF THE CITIZENS ONE ENCOUNTERS WHILE PARTICIPATING IN OUR POLITICAL PROCESS (I.E. GATHERING SIGNATURES TO SAVE THE WETLANDS)

BUMS

Bums need stuff. This goes against what you'd think. You'd think they *don't* need anything. That's the whole fun of being a bum. Wrong. They need: spare change, beer, someone to talk to, a hug, fourteen cents, a bed, an operation for their dog, a bus transfer, any extra pizza you might have, a paper clip, food stamps, to kick your ass, $400, a sock, a bottle opener, help getting their friend out of jail, a cooking mitt, a screwdriver, bolt cutters, a massage, etc. etc. One man wanted me to pull a tooth for him. Another woman tried to bite me.

BUSINESS PEOPLE

Business people can't talk to you right now. What? No. They can't talk. What? They're on their cell. What? No. Just a minute. What's that? Petition? Sign something? No. Sorry. Can't talk. Can't. Sorry. Can't.

OLD PEOPLE

Old people are old and in pain and they don't have time to listen to something they aren't going to understand anyway. They're grimacing with the pain in their back/neck/legs. They don't know where they are or what they're doing. They shuffle toward the bookstore entrance and turn their whole bodies to stare at you through the enormous lenses of their eyeglasses. They don't know why you're standing outside a bookstore with a clipboard, rattling on about swamps. But then they understand very little about the kids these days, what with their newfangled ringtones and their pants hanging halfway down their asses and their sex parties on the internet.

SOCCER MOMS

Soccer moms are very concerned. They are the most concerned people of all the people the petitioner encounters. They stop. They nod. They let their eyes rest on you. They are *very concerned.* And they are glad *for you*, that you are concerned and are doing something about it. But they don't like to sign things. Not until they read up on it more. And as soon as they do, they will sign. But they are concerned. They are very concerned. Being concerned is their job. You could never be as concerned as they are. Don't even try. Also, they're late to pick up their gifted child.

AGING HIPPIES

Aging hippies don't think you're doing it right. You're standing wrong, approaching people wrong, explaining things wrong. You obviously lack passion and true commitment. It's not the same now, not like in their day, when politics mattered and music meant something.

TOURISTS

Tourists will sign. They come to the Pacific Northwest to think about nature and reconnect with the woods and the rivers and the streams. So if you explain to them it is a petition to save nature, they get excited. They sign. They can't wait to sign. Here's the weird thing: They make up fake names and addresses. It is not clear why they do this. Maybe they think the government is keeping a secret file: people who are against destroying the world. You wouldn't want to be identified as one of those.

PEOPLE IN THEIR TWENTIES WITH TATTOOS

People in their twenties with tattoos know about your cause. They have read about it or heard something on NPR. They are very informed. Sometimes they know more about it than you do. Also, they know about other terrible things that are happening that you don't know about. "Did you hear about the nuclear waste they're dumping in the playgrounds?" And then you end up listening to them.

TEENAGERS

Teenagers don't know what the hell you're talking about. They don't. They stare at you like you're insane. Why are you *downtown*? What are you? Homeless? Don't you have parents?

THE OCCASIONAL TEENAGER WHO DOES KNOW WHAT THE HELL YOU'RE TALKING ABOUT

Every once in a while a teenager, usually a girl, comes by who *does* know what you're talking about. These are the more artsy types with messenger bags and old Vans and graphic novels under their arms. They listen to you. They sign. Sometimes they'll forge their parents' signatures for you. You kinda wish you knew them or could hang with them, but ultimately they're probably too cool or too weird. So you just smile at them and let them be on their way.

THE END

March 26

Cogs liked my petition paper. Gave me a B. I asked why not an A or at least a B+ since it was obviously hilarious (he read it to the class). He said it had no formal introduction or conclusion.

That's Cogweiller for you, always thinking outside the box.

He did write, *Glad to see you are involving yourself in your community in a positive way.*

Yeah, I gave up my drug trafficking. What did he think I did with my time?

That gave me an idea, though. Since I had my petition stuff in my bag, I asked him for a signature after class. He got a little flustered and said he couldn't do that on school grounds, it was against district policy. I said, "So we'll do it off school grounds."

This led to more awkwardness as I then had to meet Cogs after school and walk with him through the rain to his old Nissan hatchback. It was in the back parking lot, which is technically not on district property.

This was very weird. First of all, I'd never even *seen* Cogs outside of a classroom, not to mention with a ski hat on and little mittens. Also, his being elderly and all, I had to slow my pace somewhat as we walked. The other thing was: I was hoping to talk to him. I'd always been curious about the Cogman. Like what's he like on his own time? What's he into? What's his wife like? And his home life?

But walking out there, I found I couldn't start a conversation. Not at all. My role with him is: I'm the smart-ass and he's the teacher. There didn't seem to be any way to break out of that.

So I just followed along.

We got to his car. I got my petition stuff out and he signed it. I thanked him. He said nothing and got into his beater Nissan hatchback.

I watched him drive off. I felt bad we couldn't manage a conversation. But I also realized that's what's cool about him.

Cogs is a pro. No BS. No pretending we're buddies. I'm the smart-ass and he's the teacher.

You gotta respect that.

THE NEW GUY

So I'm sitting in the lounge with Jessica and some other people, and Rich Herrington comes over and starts talking about this new guy and something he did in the cafeteria. I don't know what he's talking about, but he's very excited. So is everyone else. They've all heard about this new guy. Other people join in the conversation. *Did you hear what he did? Did you hear what he said? What's his name, anyway? Where's he from?* I've never seen people at my high school get like this.

People in my high school usually don't care about anything.

As it turns out, what this new guy does — drumroll, please — is stand by the garbage cans in the cafeteria and take food people are going to throw away. He takes it off their trays, apples, rolls, whatever they don't want, whatever's edible. He's very polite about it, but people still freak out. The first time he did it, one of the cafeteria ladies with the plastic bags on her head came out and yelled at him. Then a real teacher tried to make him stop and there was a big argument. He got sent to the principal's office. But then he did it again, in direct defiance of the principal.

Which is kind of impressive, I have to admit.

People are calling him the Garbage Eater. His real name is Jedediah Strock. "Jedediah" strikes me as a pretentious name. Especially if you're not calling yourself Jed but going for the long version, which sounds like you're a pioneer homesteader or some dude out of the Bible. The garbage gathering is apparently a political statement. He's against waste. Big deal. Who isn't? Also, he has this straggly beard and long straggly hair that he pulls back with one of those girl scrunchy things. People say how intense he is. People talk about his piercing blue eyes. I'm not buying it. He sounds too obvious. Anybody can stand there eating garbage in front of the whole school.

What's your point?

I see Sadie after school, and since we're petition partners and saving the wetlands together, she comes right over and asks me if I've heard about Jedediah. I say I have. She wants to know if I've actually seen him collecting the stuff off people's trays. I haven't. "That's pretty daring, don't you think?" she asks. She's all flushed and excited about this guy. I don't answer. I ask her how the petitions went, out at the airport. She says good, they got a lot of signatures. She says she heard I did well, too, that I got sixty-five signatures. She says she couldn't believe I got so many. I say, "I'm actually quite charming when I want to be."

She says, "Yeah, when you *want* to be."

Where the hell did this Jedediah guy come from? During fourth period he sits in the middle of the main lawn, playing his guitar and *singing*. And doing

Buddhist chants. What is up with that? He wears trashed Converse low-tops that are held together with duct tape, his T-shirts are so old you can see through them, and his Hindu sheepherding jacket is shedding. He doesn't have enough facial hair to have a beard, but he has one anyway. The mystical hippie dude thing: Don't you have to be outta high school to pull that off? I heard some jocks are planning to beat him up. I feel jealous.

The jocks used to beat *me* up.

I see Sadie talking to Jedediah. God, I hate that guy. Supposedly his parents are missionaries and he lived in India for five years. Go back to frickin' India, bro. Sadie is so kissing his ass. Asking him questions. Maybe they can go into the helping-people business together. He can sing songs of love and understanding, and she can get a new bike path approved.

I hate bike paths.

I finally see him doing it. He's been forbidden to do it by every authority known to man, but there he is, during Wednesday lunch, collecting the garbage off people's trays. He does it for like thirty seconds and then Mr. Greco, the gym teacher, swoops down on him. Mr. Greco grabs Jedediah's very skinny arm and yanks him away from the garbage cans. All the apples and unopened milk cartons and stuff go spilling across the floor. Mr. Greco is an ex-Marine. He grabs the Garbage Eater by the back of his shirt and marches him toward the principal's office. But here's the killer. As he's being led away, people begin to clap. Everyone in the cafeteria starts clapping and standing up. Soon the whole cafeteria is on their feet giving him a standing ovation, as Mr. Greco practically rips his shirt off. I have to stand up or look like a total jerk.

I don't clap, though.

In the meantime, while the Garbage Eater is getting all the attention at school, I'm stuck downtown trying to get crazy people to sign my stupid petition. That's my own demented sense of honor. I said I'd do the petitions, so I do them. One good thing: I finally meet Alice Weitzman. She's the head of Save the Wetlands. She actually comes down to my corner to see the kid who got sixty-five signatures on his first day. I thought she was another street person when she first walked up to me. But she introduced herself and she had this funny way about her. You sort of instantly want to help her. But a lot of good that does me. I'm still standing in the street getting signatures, while Sadie is somewhere else, getting all sparkle-eyed over Jedediah. Everyone thinks he's so rad. They love that he keeps doing the garbage thing no matter how many times they bust him. Of course his parents have been called. That's the latest news everyone is buzzing about.

What will the missionary parents do?

*   *   *

I don't think Sadie is really in love with Jedediah. But who knows? He keeps getting in trouble and now his parents are involved. Apparently, his mother screamed at Mr. Brown about how racist our school is. Sadie is all worked up about it. People are saying Jedediah has a First Amendment right to express himself. Collecting garbage is freedom of speech. Other people (me) think he's a show-off. Someone interviewed him for the school paper and it turned out he has been thrown out of a couple different schools for similar escapades. The teachers all know he isn't hurting anything, but at the same time they can't let him do stuff he's been told not to do.

I can just imagine Mr. Brown sitting in his office rolling his eyes.

I see the Garbage Eater and Sadie sitting out on the main lawn during lunch. His guitar is lying gently on the grass, he's sitting cross-legged, his ancient Converse duct-taped to his feet. Sadie's doing her "attentive" pose, her "help me be a better person" posture. So I decide to go see for myself. Maybe I've been too harsh on this guy. We are on the same side, after all. Probably Sadie will tell him about our petition. I'm the guy who got sixty-five signatures on my first day. So I walk over and say hi and sit down, and Jedediah pretends I'm not there. He's too busy going on and on about India, the conditions there, the poor, the way his parents taught him to never give in to structure or authority or meaningless directives. He is a very earnest dude. I try to roll with it. I nod and agree that starvation is bad. But he barely acknowledges me. He is totally focused on Sadie. They are bonding in a deep do-gooder trance of self-righteousness and high self-esteem energies. The bell's about to ring and I have to go, so I say good-bye and stand up. They barely notice. Sadie could have helped. She could have said: "Jedediah, this is James. He's helping me save the wetlands." But she doesn't.

Sixty-five signatures in one day. Keep that in mind, Mr. Strock.

A PARTIAL LIST AND DESCRIPTION OF GIRLS WHO WOULD PROBABLY LIKE TO SIT WITH *ME* ON A LAWN SOMEWHERE AND SHARE HIGH SELF-ESTEEM ENERGIES

JESSICA CARLUCCI

Jessica is awesome. And quite beautiful. Sometimes when the light hits her hair, it is the nicest, softest shade of brown. I bet she wouldn't mind doing something of a semi-romantic nature. We might have to skip the sitting in the grass part, though. She doesn't like to get her clothes dirty.

HEATHER LANGHORN

I don't talk about Heather much but her locker is two down from mine and she likes good music and dresses cool. She'd probably want to hang out sometime if I asked her.

CASSANDRA BENSON

Cassandra is a friend of Renee's, who once started talking to me while Gabe was talking to Renee. We had a nice conversation. That was like a month ago, though.

WHAT'S MY PROBLEM?

What is my problem with girls? I go to a huge public high school. How can I not find someone to at least hang out with? I'm seventeen years old!

OTHER SCHOOLS

Other schools is what some people resort to when they can't get anywhere with our girls. They start talking about the mythical Lincoln girls. Or the hot babes at Wilson. "The hot babes at Wilson are not uptight like our girls," they say. "They're always ready to party and they'll make out with anyone."

Sure they will.

THE GIRL AT THE BUS STOP

There's a girl who is sometimes at my bus stop going home from school. She is older, probably nineteen or twenty. I think she works at the mall. She smiles at me sometimes. I bet she'd want to hang out. I'd need her to turn off her iPod, though, so I could ask her.

THE EVIL ONE SPEAKS

I'm upstairs staring at my math homework and my dad
appears at my door.

DAD: So your mother said she talked to you about
     college?

ME: ——

DAD: What are your plans in that department?

ME: ——

DAD: Do you have any preferences? Any areas in
     particular you're interested in?

ME: ——

DAD: You know I've always thought law school might
     be a good option for you. Down the road.

ME: ???

DAD: You know, this is your future we're talking
     about. This is not the time to play out some
     resentment you have against your mother
     and me.

ME: ! ! !

DAD: Contrary to what you think, we're very open
     about this and we want you to go somewhere
     you would feel comfortable.

ME: ——

DAD: Will you think about this?

ME: ——

DAD: All right, then . . .

ME: ——

April 8

Sadie is getting more involved in the Garbage Eater's situation at our school. She and several members of the Activist Club had a meeting with the principal and made a big fuss about our rights as students to make political statements. Why can't Jedediah take food off other people's trays if it doesn't affect anyone else? The principal claims it's a health risk, that Jedediah might get sick from eating other people's food. Sadie's crew did not consider this an adequate response. Everyone is very worked up about it. People are discussing possible protests. Jedediah Strock remains the talk of the school.

April 9

Sadie and the Activist Club people have developed a plan to support the Garbage Eater. We're all going to share food off each other's plates one day in the cafeteria. As a protest. This was not Sadie's idea, it was another girl's. This Share Our Food Day is supposedly going to happen on Thursday.

Meanwhile, an editorial appeared by Sadie's friend Jill Kantor.

BEWARE THE GARBAGE EATER!

A terrible new threat has appeared in our cafeteria. He is the so-called "Garbage Eater." This sick individual has dared disrupt our normal lunchroom business with his outrageous claims that we are wasting food. Not only that, he actually takes the food we are wasting and doesn't let us waste it! How dare he! It is our food. We can waste it if we want!

One freshman we spoke to was already deeply confused by his dangerous political message. "I thought we were supposed to throw our food away, but there was this guy and he was like, 'Do you want that?' And I was like, 'No.' And he took it off my tray. I think he's going to eat it later. Can you do that?" The answer, frosh-person, is no, you cannot!

The Garbage Eater is poisoning the minds of our underclassmen. He is also getting extra milk and tater tots and corn bread! Why should he get a free lunch, just because the rest of us are throwing ours away?

I enjoyed this so much I tried to find Jill Kantor and tell her, but I couldn't figure out where her locker was.

April 11

Gabe and I went to the cafeteria early today to make sure we didn't miss the Share Our Food protest. We sat there while everyone waited for the word to share food. The teachers all knew about it anyway. They'd already said they weren't going to do anything. Finally, the moment came and everyone "shared" food. Mostly they just touched each other's food. Gabe and I switched our cookies back and forth. Overall it was not what I would call an effective protest. But it seemed to make people feel better.

SAVING THE WETLANDS

Finally, the stupid Save the Wetlands thing pays off.
There's a meeting at Alice Weitzman's house for all the
people participating. Sadie comes by and picks me up.

I shouldn't say it's stupid. Everyone loves the pond
and the woods around Carl Haney's house. One old guy
wrote a thing on the STW website about how there used
to be a half-dozen ponds in the area when he was a kid.
He and his buddies would ride their bikes around with
their fishing poles tied to the handlebars. They'd catch
bass in the ponds. Now this is the only one left, and it's
getting so polluted there probably aren't any bass in it
anyway.

Sadie and I pull into the driveway at Alice's house.
It's a big house and there's fancy appetizers and wine
and all that. I hear someone say Alice's husband is a
high-powered lawyer. She's great, though, Alice, padding
around in her slippers and her flowing clothes and a
goofy hat. It's mostly older people in attendance, but
there are some younger people here and there. A couple
of cats wander around.

We get down to business. The group of us sit in folding chairs in her living room. Alice stands in front and
tells us what's going on with the petitions. She tells us
how many signatures we got and thanks the petitioners
individually. She reads our names and asks us to identify
ourselves. Most people wave a hand, but when she calls

my name, I stand up and bow deeply. Everyone thinks that's funny. Everyone except Sadie.

After the meeting, Sadie drives me home. I'm hoping we can hang out or talk a little. That doesn't seem to be happening, but at the last minute she asks if I mind driving by the pond to check it out.

"No," I say. "I don't mind."

We pull onto the little dirt road and run right into a new metal gate. These developer guys don't waste any time. We get out for a closer look. The gate is a long metal bar with a padlock hanging off one end. It's only to stop cars. We can still walk in. Sadie isn't sure she wants to. We have school the next day and it's already ten. It's also really deserted, and there are big new NO TRESPASSING signs all over the place. I convince Sadie we'll be okay. We both want to see what else they've done.

We crawl under the metal bar and walk down the road. The moon is out, so we can see pretty well. We follow the couple curves of the road and get to the pond. It's about fifty yards across. It looks like it always did. Mushy. Swampy. Smelly. Sadie looks around at everything. I pick up a stick and throw it into the water.

"Doesn't seem like they've done anything to it yet," Sadie says.

"How do you even drain a pond?" I ask.

"You pump all the water out and fill it up with dirt. Weren't you listening to Alice?"

I shrug.

I start walking slowly through the grass around the edge. Sadie follows. We go a little ways and something jumps into the water. A frog, probably. Sadie stops. Then something else scurries into the bushes behind us. Sadie looks at me.

"Probably just a raccoon," I say. "Or a possum."

Sadie hates possums. We keep going, but she stays close behind me. At one point I hold her hand and help her jump over some muck.

We pick our way along the trail that circles the pond. It's more grown over than I remember. I guess nobody is coming here anymore.

About halfway around is the bonfire spot. There's a clearing, with a log where people sit and an ashy burn pit surrounded by rocks. A half-melted plastic six-pack ring is sticking out of it, and there's some beer cans around, quite a few beer cans.

"Why do people always get drunk in places like this?" Sadie asks me. "And light fires?"

"That's what people do," I say. "They start chemical reactions."

Sadie stops and stares at the pond. It looks different from this side. It's awfully small as bodies of water go. And it smells. I wonder if it's even worth saving. I don't say that, though.

"Do you remember when we came here?" Sadie says.

"We came here a couple times."

"Yeah, we did."

I step closer to her. I suddenly want to do something. I'm not sure what. Comfort her? Put my arm around her?

Before I can do either, she turns away. She walks to the edge of the pond and looks out.

I pick up another stick and throw it in the water.

We head back. I remember that if you go all the way around, you hit a patch of black muck that *really* smells. So we return the way we came. We reach the road and walk toward the car in silence. I help her under the metal gate. But at the moment when we split up, to go to the different car doors, she stops. I almost walk into her.

"Do you mind if we hang out for one second?" she says. "I want to look at everything."

"Okay."

She looks. I look, too. We're standing in front of her dad's car. We're about two feet from each other.

"The moon is nice," I say.

"Think how many people have come here over the years," she says. "Think how many people had their first kiss here."

"We didn't," I say.

"I'm not talking about us."

"We had our first kiss in your driveway," I say. "I was on my bike."

"Why are you bringing that up?"

"No reason."

"You've seemed kinda weird all night."

"So?" I say. "I am weird."

Sadie stares at a stand of tall evergreen trees to our right. "I just want to look around. I want to feel this place. I want to know what I'm fighting for."

"Do you think it will make any difference?" I say. "If the people bought it, they can drain it. They've drained all the other ponds."

"So you want to give up? Why did you bother getting all those signatures?"

"Why do you think?" I say.

She stares at me in the dark. Then turns away.

I pick up a rock and throw it at the gate. I hit the metal bar on the first try, a lucky shot. It makes a ringing metallic sound.

"I don't even know what difference it's gonna make," I say. "We're all gonna fry anyway."

"You know, I've really missed your pessimistic worldview," says Sadie. "I miss that wonderful sense of doom you bring to things."

This statement sparks something in me. I watch her face in the dark. I want to kiss her. The sensation starts like an itch, like a tiny urge, and then blossoms into this incredible need that I can barely contain. I take a step toward her. I'm going to do it.

But then I decide not to, and I pick up another rock.

"Realists are never happy . . . ," I say, throwing it.

"Is that what you are, a realist?"

"I think so."

"Then what am I?"

"You're . . . ," I say. "You're more of a . . ."

But I can't finish the sentence. I face her. I don't want to talk anymore. I want to be in that place again, that place of her.

"I'm more of a — ?" she says, but her voice has dropped to a whisper. She doesn't want to talk either. The talking is over. This is the crucial moment. It's now or never.

I go for the kiss. I step toward her, grip her shoulder, aim my mouth at hers.

I press my lips against hers.

She lets me do this. She lets me kiss her, and I do. But when I try to coax her mouth open, she won't. And she isn't going to put her arms around me either. She isn't going to do anything.

That's not good.

I stop. I open my eyes.

She pulls herself away from me. "What, *on earth*, are you doing?" she says in the darkness.

"Nothing. I just —"

"You just kissed me!"

"I thought you —"

"*What are you doing!?*"

"I didn't mean —"

"Do you still *like* me?" she asks, point blank.

"I . . . I don't know."

"You don't *know?*"

"I do, I guess. I must," I hear myself say.

She stands there staring at me. Then she touches her lips with her fingertips, as if to check that they're still there.

It's dark enough that we can't really see each other's facial expressions, which is probably for the best.

James Hoff
Junior AP English
Mr. Cogweiller
ASSIGNMENT: *describe a group or organization you have been a part of*

MY LIFE AS A TEENAGER

Being a teen is an exciting time for a young person. It is the first stage of your life when you're associated with a decade. You start off as a "baby." Then you're a "child." Then you graduate onto the conveyor belt of decades. First it's your "teens." Then it's your "twenties." Then your "thirties," your "forties," your "fifties," and so on until you die.

People who actually are teens think of the word as old-fashioned, a bit cheesy, but they are still attracted to things labeled "teen." This is because they are curious about what other people think "teens" are supposed to be like and what they're supposed to do. They are not quite sure what a "teen" is, even though they technically are one.

Despite the cheese factor, the word "teen" does help young people find each other. Certain channels on TV are for "teens." At the bookstore, there is a "Teen" section. At one vacation spot I know, there is a place called "the TeenZone" where they have French fries and video games and booths to hang out in. Teens like to "hang out." They also like hoodies and lip gloss and Skittles. Teen girls like shopping and TV shows about other teen girls having lavish sweet sixteen parties. Teen boys like blowing stuff up.

Teens, being younger, are envied by adults. Teens have longer to live. They can goof around more. They don't have as many cares and worries. Also, they are cooler than adults. And better looking. They are better dancers.

But teens are also easily confused. They don't understand the world. They have strong chemicals going through them that give them acne and make them sexually frustrated. Teen boys masturbate frequently. They can't help it. You can pretty much grab any teen boy and accuse him of being a "masturbator" and you will be right.

Do teen girls masturbate? No one knows.

Teens are at the beginning of life. For this reason, one of their main characteristics is their inexperience. Teens spend most of their time learning to do things: how to study, how to hold a job, how to not get caught masturbating. But since the teen is so inexperienced, problems arise and the teen is not prepared.

Also, certain things that are inherently flawed appear to the teen to be perfect. For instance, drinking. The teen drinks multiple beers, plays air guitar, hangs his ass out the window of his friend's car but then is shocked when he wakes up with a hangover and angry parents.

Or driving. The teen borrows Mom's car, drives fast, plays European Race Car Driver, but then is shocked when the car ends up in the ditch.

Or love. The teen falls in love, wanders the streets in ecstasy, and then is shocked when that love falters for no apparent reason. When this happens, the teen thinks he can fix it. The teen does not know that some things cannot be fixed. This leads the teen to try impossible things.

For this reason, let us have some sympathy for the teen. He wants to do good, but he doesn't know how. He wants to love, but something always goes wrong. He wants to fix the relationship because he loves the girl. The girl loves him. And yet something is broken. The teen digs down into the relationship to find that broken thing, to find it and fix it. But that thing is unfindable. The teen must face the horrible truth: The world is not going to give him what he wants. Even things that appear right in front of him, that seem easily graspable, even these things are, in reality, just outside his reach.

The End

April 12

Slinking around school today. Hiding in the library. I
don't know what I'm afraid of exactly. Sadie's not going
to tell anyone what happened at the pond. It's still so
embarrassing, though. I'm afraid to show my face. . . .
Gabe is being a good friend, walking with me in and
out of the parking lot. He's got his license, so that's good.
Not that I enjoy riding around in the Ford Expedition,
which he now drives to school. I guess it's easier to
criticize a Ford Expedition when you don't need it
to avoid the ex-girlfriend you tried to kiss in a moment
of reckless stupidity.

Gabe has refrained from saying "I told you so" about
Sadie. But he did tell me so.

He's also been getting on me about my dad's car
offer. Needless to say, he thinks I should take it.

"Dude, your parents are offering you a car, and
college. That's two awesome things for nothing!"

"But I hate cars."

"Dude, get a hybrid," said Gabe. "Get a Prius. Get a
freakin' electric go-cart if you have to. Take the deal!"

One thought I had: I could call Sadie and apologize. That
would appear very mature, very civilized.

Or I could just go throw myself off a bridge, like a
real seventeen-year-old.

Or I could just grow a new humiliation zit on my chin,
which is apparently what my pores have decided to do.

April 14

Bored and girl-less, Gabe and I drive around. It's Saturday
night and we've got nothing to do. We go to Fred
Meyer's. We sit in the car and listen to the radio and
watch people in the parking lot.

Then Gabe gets a call. It's Renee. There's a party
somewhere. Gabe is very excited about this. He still likes
Renee. I don't think that's ever going to happen but I keep
quiet. We start up the monster engine and off we go.

So we get there and the party is at this senior girl's house
we don't know. We go in and it's kind of crowded and we
find Renee and some other people downstairs, playing
foosball. It's pretty much a jock/prep crowd. I do my best
to hang, for Gabe's sake.

Then Stephanie appears. Stephanie, from Disco
Bowling. I haven't seen her in a while. She looks good,
though. She's wearing dark eye makeup and a cute skirt.
I think, *Maybe I could go out with her.* She's attractive.
She's a girl. She thought I was vain, I seem to
remember. Well, that will give us something to talk
about.

"Hey," I say, handing her a Coke someone just
handed me.

"Thank god," she says, putting down the Bud Light
she was carrying and taking the Coke. "I hate Bud
Light."

"Me, too."

"Why do they even have it here? We're in high school. Can't we drink normal beer, like normal high school students?"

"Maybe Bud Light is normal beer."

We stand there and watch people play foosball. Stephanie might be a little drunk. "So what's up with you these days?" she asks me.

"I'm looking for a new girlfriend," I answer. "Gabe is making me."

"Did you have an old girlfriend?"

"I did. Sadie Kinnell."

"Sadie Kinnell?" she says, surprised. "I know her. She's always doing things to save the world."

"That's the one."

Stephanie sips her Coke. We look at each other. Stephanie has quite a bit of eye mascara on. She's definitely drunk.

I *feel* drunk. And I feel like talking. So I do. "I tried to get back with her," I say. "I tried to kiss her. I just sorta went for it. I thought she would be into it. But she wasn't."

"Guys always do that," says Stephanie, waving at someone. "They always go for the kiss at the wrong moment. Or they don't go for it at all."

"Yeah . . ."

"Why did you guys break up, anyways?"

"I'm too depressing," I say. "My brain. It's full of darkness."

"Oh."

"I think about what you said sometimes," I tell her. "The thing about shyness being a form of vanity."

"Oh yeah. I remember that." She drinks more Coke.

"I think you might be right about that," I say.

"Of course I am."

"So what should I do? How can I make myself more likeable?"

"You could dress normal. Didn't you used to cut up your clothing? That's too weird. You can't do stuff like that."

"Yeah, but what about my brain?"

"What about it?" she says. "Drink more. Or get some meds or whatever." She looks at the Coke can I gave her. "This doesn't have any alcohol in it."

"No," I say.

She spots a passing senior with a Heineken. "Hey, cutie," she says, grabbing his arm. "Where did you get that?"

He points to a downstairs refrigerator. "Thank you!" she says. To me: "You want one?"

"Nah, I'm good," I say. She disappears in the direction of the refrigerator and I turn back toward the foosball game. Everyone's shouting and jumping around as the little ball bounces around. They look like monkeys in a zoo.

I stand there and pretend to watch. I think about Jill Kantor. That was a funny editorial she wrote. I wonder what she does on Friday nights. I wonder what sort of books she reads.

April 16

It's been five days since I tried to kiss Sadie at the pond.
I haven't seen her since. Then this morning, in the
cafeteria, we finally ran into each other. I gave her my
most humble, apologetic smile. She didn't accept it. Her
eyes bounced right off me and she kept on walking.

After that I went to fifth period and sat in the back.
The teacher started to talk and all I could think was: *Oh
my god, I have lost Sadie again.* Tears came into my eyes.
I thought of stuff we did when we first got together, how
we used to have coffee at Café Artiste and walk around
and talk about the Russian Revolution, while the yellow
leaves fell around us. And then these last months,
starting back at the library, how good it felt to talk to her,
how happy I was to be around her again. And the feeling
of having a shot. I felt like I had a shot with her. I really
did. BUT I SCREWED IT UP. AGAIN. She is not getting
back with me. It is not happening.

The teacher called on me. I was like, "What do *you*
want?" I mean, I didn't say that. But I might as well have.

April 23

Went to see Ms. Flowers today. She's our college
counselor. She wanted to see my list of schools I was
interested in. I didn't have one.

So then we talked about other stuff, and what was
going on with me. Whatever that's supposed to mean.

I told her I didn't know if I wanted to go to college.
She batted her long eyelashes at me and said, "But what
would you do instead?"

That is an excellent question.

April 26

Jedediah Strock got expelled today for crawling around in the dumpster outside the cafeteria. Everyone was talking about it. People don't get expelled from Evergreen very often, so it's kind of a big deal. Everyone was totally pissed at first, like it's *sooo* not right, it's *sooo* not fair. But then this sense of gloom settled over the whole school, as people realized he'd left the administration no choice. He made them do it. He'd forced their hand.

I saw one of the Activist Club girls in the hall. She looked like she was about to cry. I'm sure Sadie is all over this right now. I'm sure she and Jedediah are off somewhere having secret, impassioned conversations. I can imagine him comforting her, telling her it is okay, he will live to fight again.

Maybe if I was more like him, she would want me back. If I stood up more for what I believed in. The problem is, I don't believe in anything.

April 27

By some strange coincidence, I happen to be in the hallway when Jedediah gets escorted out of school for the last time. He'd cleaned out his locker and was walking through the hall with an armful of books and his old Tibetan backpack. Our vice principal and some security guy were with him.

He looked very heroic, very much like a martyr for the cause. It's weird, though, because class had already started and there weren't any people in the hall to see him go. Maybe they planned it that way. I was the only one there because I was blowing off study hall. It was kind of an important moment, and everyone was missing it.

I saw it, though. Poor guy. I wonder what goes on in his head? No one really knows him. I wonder if he's ever had a girlfriend. You'd think he'd have his pick of the Activist Club girls. Probably he won't lower himself to hook up with girls. He's too pure. Or maybe that's all he's after. Maybe the whole Garbage Eater thing is a way to get chicks.

Jedediah Strock: mystery man.

April 30

Back entrance, after school, Sadie is standing against the wall, waiting for me.

SADIE: James?

ME (*surprised*): Hey —

SADIE: I need to talk to you. Do you have a second?

ME: Sure.

SADIE: Come over here.

ME (*following her around the building*): What do you want to talk about?

SADIE (*stopping*): What do you think?

ME: I don't know.

SADIE: How about what happened at the pond?

ME: Okay.

SADIE: Why did you do that?

ME: What do you mean?

SADIE: You can't just kiss people randomly, you know.

ME: Why not? Is it against the law?

SADIE: Because it freaks people out!

ME: Sorry.

SADIE: You totally . . . I was totally . . . in shock!

ME: I didn't mean to —

SADIE: And now what am I supposed to do? Can we even hang out? Can I trust you? Can we even be friends?

ME: I don't know. Maybe we can't.

SADIE: *Maybe we can't?* That's your answer?

ME: Well, what do you expect me to say!?

SADIE: That's the other thing about you. You are a total quitter. You just give up the minute things get difficult.

ME: Like what things?

SADIE: Like being friends! Or anything. You can't just grab me in the middle of the night and do something like that and not have any kind of . . . explanation.

ME: What do you want me to say?

SADIE: God. I can't believe you sometimes. And we're supposed to be saving the pond!

ME: Maybe that's how I felt.

SADIE: And you don't have anything else to say about it? Except that?

ME: No. Not really.

SADIE: All right then. So I guess I should just ask the obvious question. If I do, will you answer it truthfully?

ME: I'll try.

SADIE: Okay then.

ME: Okay.

SADIE (*shifting her stance*): Do you still like me?

ME: You already asked me that.

SADIE: But you didn't answer!

ME: Okay, I'll answer. I . . . I do. I mean —

SADIE: See! You're not answering again! You're being wishy-washy. You're being noncommittal!

ME: Okay. Yes. I do like you still. What do you want from me? It wasn't my idea to break up.

SADIE: And whose idea was it? Mine?

ME: It seemed like it was. You brought it up.

SADIE: It was mutual! I thought we agreed that it was.

ME: Maybe you did.

SADIE: So did you!

ME: Okay. Maybe I did. But maybe I was wrong. Maybe that's not what I wanted.

SADIE (*shaking her head*): This isn't the way this is supposed to happen. You know that, don't you? Even if we do still like each other. This is not the way to handle the situation!

ME: How am I supposed to know how to handle it? I don't want to get hurt again.

SADIE: I wouldn't do that to you. . . .

ME: Yes, you would. You wouldn't try to. But you would.

SADIE: Well, what about me? You're the one kissing people with no warning! What about my feelings?

ME: Your feelings? Are you kidding me? I would do anything for you. You're the only thing I care about in this entire world.

SADIE: ——

ME: ——

SADIE (*catching her breath*): Wow. I can't believe
we're having this conversation.

ME: Me neither.

SADIE: This is really weird.

ME: I know.

SADIE: So what do we do now?

ME: I don't know.

SADIE: Well, I don't know either.

ME: I guess we should just try to . . . figure something out.

MOVIE

We go to a movie that weekend. Sadie and I. We decide
that's a low-key, relatively safe thing to do, considering
our situation. We're just gonna try it. See how it goes. It's
an experiment.

She picks me up in her dad's Camry and we drive to
the cineplex. Everything's cool. I'm excited, and a little
nervous. I'm wearing my favorite deck shoes and my
sweater with the elbows cut out for good luck. We drive
through my neighborhood. I roll down my window and
breathe in the soft spring air. I watch the houses pass,
the streetlights move by in rhythm.

It's a little strange, sitting beside Sadie and knowing
that this is pretty much a date. But I'm okay. I'm loose.
I'm hanging in.

On the main road, we talk about stuff. She tells me
about this fellowship she's got where she's going up to
British Columbia for eight weeks this summer, to help
build an eco-park. You build the eco-park during the
day and at night they teach you forestry and conservation
and stuff like that. It sounds amazing. Also, her older
brother is flunking out of Berkeley. He doesn't want to
go to med school now. Her parents are not happy about
that. She talked to him and he said he wants to take a
year off and do music, since that's his first love.

She asks me about my family, and I tell her my parents are freaking out about my lack of interest in college.
I tell her about the deal my dad is offering me. Go to

college, get a car. She laughs when she hears that. I laugh, too.

At the theater, we go inside, get popcorn, and find a place to sit. It's been almost one year since we broke up. May 12th, it was. A Tuesday. It was a relatively orderly breakup. No crying. No pleading. We were both more relieved than anything. We sat on her parents' steps outside her house and talked it through. I remember picking at the laces of my tennis shoe for most of it. It *was* mutual. That part is true. I wanted . . . I don't know what . . . to run around with my guy friends more, to meet other girls, to have different experiences. She wanted freedom, too. Girls don't think of it that way, but it's true. She wanted to meet new people, do new things, grow into a different person.

We had to give stuff back to each other. Sadie was a big mixer of stuff. We had a lot of crap at each other's house. So we had to sort that out. Also, she offered to make me a copy of the love letter I wrote her at Christmas from Costa Rica, but I said no, I didn't want it.

Then, a week later, I ran into her mom at Fred Meyer's. Of course, I stopped and talked to her like I always did. But then as I stood there making conversation, I remembered that I wasn't going out with her daughter anymore. We didn't have to talk anymore. I was like, "Okay, Mrs. Kinnell, I should probably get going." I cried all the way home. It was the first time I cried. It was the first time I truly understood what I had lost.

*   *   *

In the movie theater, I eat my popcorn. Sadie eats hers. She puts her feet up on the seat in front of her, which she always used to do. I do the same. The weird thing about this is we already know everything the other person is going to do. We've done all of this before.

The movie comes on. It's a thriller with some sort of plot twist that I miss, so I'm confused the whole time. Sadie doesn't seem to get it either. But we sit there. We watch the car chase scene. Stuff blows up at the end.

Afterward, we walk around the mall and go back to her car. We're both thinking, *Now what do we do?* At the same time, there's no real pressure. Like what's the worst that could happen? We're gonna break up? We already broke up. We're broken up now.

We get in the Camry. We both seem older somehow, and we act older around each other. There isn't that electricity that comes when you're out with someone you barely know. Not that I've done that so many times. Twice, actually: Kristine the Goth Chick and Lucy Branch.

A strange thing happens then. I think about Lucy Branch, who I never think about. I wonder how she's doing. Good, I hope. She was nice. I wonder if she feels weird about going to that French movie that time. I should remember to say hi to her in the hall sometime. I never really see her, though.

Sadie pulls out of the parking lot. I'm not saying anything and she's not sure what the plan is, so she says, "I should probably get back. I have that big history test. . . ."

"Yeah, I have a paper due," I say. We drive a little more. But then I start to feel like I did at the pond, like I want to kiss her, like if I don't kiss her, I'm gonna die.

"You don't by chance . . . feel like . . . ," I say.

"What?" she says.

"You wanna go check out the pond for a minute?"

"Okay," she says.

We drive to the pond. We pull in and the metal gate is open. That's odd.

Sadie cautiously drives down the dirt road and slows down as we near the water. We both look around to see what else has happened. That's when we see a row of property stakes stuck in the hillside to our left. Each one has a bright pink ribbon tied to the top.

"Here they come," Sadie murmurs.

I say nothing. But I stare at them, too. The stakes. The concept of private property. They *are* coming. And when they're done, there will be no pond, no trees, no nothing — just spanky new houses, with chemical lawns and SUVs parked out front.

Sadie turns off the engine and we sit for a moment. Frogs croak in the warm night. The property stakes seem to change the mood between us. I still want to kiss her. But there's something I want to do first.

We get out of the car. Sadie stands by her door, her arms crossed. I go after the stakes.

I hop over the ditch, crawl up the muddy hill, and try to yank the top stake out of the ground. It won't come out. I have to work it back and forth. While I'm doing that, Sadie crawls up the hill and tries pulling on one herself. I finally pull mine out, then break another one, then pull out two more. Sadie has managed to pull out a couple as well.

When we've uprooted all of them, we throw them in the ditch.

"That's not going to do much," Sadie says, wiping the dirt off her hands.

"Yeah, but it feels good," I say back.

We both jump back over the ditch. We walk back toward the car. Both our shoes are caked with mud. I try to kick the mud off mine.

That's when I notice Sadie watching me. She's staring at me.

"What?" I say.

"Nothing," she answers.

"You don't approve of my methods?"

"Have you ever approved of mine?"

I smile. I go back to my shoes. I scrape the mud off with a stick.

She holds her foot out and I scrape the mud off hers, too. She steadies herself by gripping my shoulder.

We are standing very close. I hold her ankle. I clean her shoe.

When I stand up, she's there, those blue eyes are watching me, waiting for me in the dark.

I kiss her.

She is ready for it this time. She welcomes it. She kisses me back.

We separate briefly, letting the weight of what is happening move through us.

Then I slip my hands inside her coat, grip the curve of her waist, pull her closer still. Our foreheads rest together. We kiss more, slowly, intimately, breathing each other's air.

Eventually, we end up in the Camry, in the backseat. We really start to make out then. She gets like I've never seen her, breathless and pressing against me. I am getting like that, too. We're older now; we know what we want.

"This is getting a little intense," she finally gasps, in the quiet of the backseat.

"I know," I breathe.

"Should we stop?"

"I don't know."

"I feel like . . . ," she whispers. "Like maybe . . ."

We keep going. We go and go and go.

"Do you have something?" I finally say, my shirt off, my face damp and hot.

"What do you mean?"

"You know."

"I don't —"

"We need something."

She sighs. She breathes. "In my coat. Hand me my coat."

She has a condom in her coat. This is a huge surprise.

But I say nothing. I reach into the front seat, find the coat, and hand it to her. She untangles it, digs through the pocket. She finds the condom. She hands it to me.

I fumble with the plastic wrapper. I can't open it.

"Here." She takes it from me, tears it open, and hands it back.

I fumble with it more. She watches me. "Is it on right?"

"I don't know," I gasp.

"It has to be on right."

"I think it is —"

She checks it. It's okay. She puts her head back. "Oh God," she whispers to herself.

We do it. I kiss her while we do it. I hold her, I stroke her hair. I lose myself in her. I can't believe how good it feels. I am lost to the world. I am in another place. . . .

Afterward, a deep silence settles over us. I lift my head and stare into her eyes. I touch her flushed face, stroke her mussed hair, kiss the side of her cheek.

I rest my head on her shoulder and she strokes my neck.

Outside, the pond sits silently, waiting to be drained.

PART
6

AFTERMATH

The next morning, I wake up in my bed. It's Saturday morning. I stare at the ceiling. I'm not a virgin anymore.

I lift my head and look around my room. Everything looks pretty much the same. Same posters. Same Post-it notes stuck to the wall over my desk. Same dirty clothes spilling out of the closet. I look at my arm, at the back of my hand. It all looks the same.

I get out of bed and go to the bathroom. It's the same bathroom I've been using my whole life. Libby has left her Flintstones toothpaste out. I put it away.

Some people are in a hurry to grow up. They can't wait to get to high school, to get their license, to get their first kiss, their first girlfriend, their first sexual experience. I'm not like that. I mean, I'm glad to move forward with my life. But it makes me sad, too. Once you move on, you can't go back.

I look at myself in the mirror. I don't look different. I guess I'm not really different. Maybe losing your virginity isn't such a big deal after all.

But then I think of Sadie. I remember how she kissed me, how her body felt underneath me. The whole situation with us, we're not even going out. So why did we do that?

Sadie's changed so much. She has sex with people now.

So do I. Now.

I go downstairs. Mom is gone. Dad is in his study. Libby is on the phone in the TV room. I make myself some cereal and try to eat it. I can't. I don't feel like myself, not at all.

I can't stay in the house. My bike's lying on its side in the garage, I pick it up and pedal down the street to Shari's. I assume I'm going to calmly order their $5.99 breakfast, but as soon as the waitress brings me my coffee, I see that is impossible. I drink half the coffee, pay, leave.

I don't know where to go, or what to do.

I find myself at the library, but it's Saturday and it's crowded with people and I can't imagine going in. I stop for a second, though, and sit on the bench outside. I think about Sadie more. I love her. I loved her. I don't know what I feel. She has changed so much. So have I. We had sex. When you have sex with people, it's different. It's not just messing around. It's the big leagues. It's playing for keeps. Jesus, *what have I done?*

But no, I'm glad. I guess I am. I don't know. I don't know anything.

I go home. There's a basketball game on TV, which I try to watch. I see nothing. I couldn't care less. I go upstairs and sit in my room and I feel like I'm going to cry.

Later, I call Gabe. He asks me what's up. I tell him.

"Dude," he says very quietly.

"I know," I say. I don't talk very long. There's not much to say. I hang up.

All day, I have thought about when I should call Sadie. I have to call her today, that seems clear enough. But whenever I think that, I immediately think, "I'll call her later."

Now it is later. I look at the numbers on the phone. I don't call her. I go upstairs and get in my bed. I stare at the ceiling. I know what it feels like to be in love. I've been lucky in that way. I've been in love. But what this feeling is, I don't know. It's not regret exactly. Or sadness. But it's not joy or happiness either.

Maybe it's knowledge. Maybe it's my first glimpse of the truth of grown-up relationships.

Whatever it is, it is older than I am. It is ancient. It is something from the very deepest parts of life.

May 7

ALICE: Hello? May I speak with James Hoff, please?

ME: This is James.

ALICE: Hi, James. This is Alice Weitzman.

ME: Hey, Alice.

ALICE: I wanted to call and personally let you know that the city council has chosen not to allow our petition in their hearings.

ME: Are you serious? Can they do that?

ALICE: Yes, unfortunately they can. As you know, we barely had the required number of signatures, and many of those were challenged. That's something the city council does when groups don't have an overwhelming volume of signatures. You really need to have twice as many signatures as are required by law.

ME: Oh.

ALICE: There's nothing we can do about it now. We didn't have enough publicity. I tried calling a friend at Channel 2, but she said it's not important enough, it's just a pond and some woods, there's no principle at stake.

ME: Why does there have to be a principle? Can't it just be a pond and some woods?

ALICE: The press is like that. It's hard to hold people's attention. We knew that — we just didn't have time to work around it. Anyway, it's only one setback, this is a battle being fought on many fronts.

ME: Yeah, but that sucks.

ALICE: I know. That's why I called. To let you know how much we appreciate your help.

ME: I can't believe they can do that.

ALICE: Well, they can, and that's what happens sometimes. My main hope is that you might be willing to petition for us in the future. You seem to have a talent for it.

ME: Sure. Of course. So what happens to the pond now?

ALICE: The pond is already drained. They did it over the weekend.

ME: They did?

ALICE: Yes.

ME: Jeez.

ALICE: I hope you'll stick with us, James. We always need people, but we especially need young people. Young people give life to things. They give people hope.

May 12

It's been awkward sitting with Sadie in the cafeteria.
She's made a lot of new friends since last year. The
Activist Club girls. Jill Kantor from the paper. These two
guys from her Spanish class who are from Central
America. I don't really know any of these people.

Gabe tries to help out. He sits with us, but he really
wants to sit with Renee and keeps looking over in that
direction. And anyway, it's getting close to the end of the
year and people are bored with the cafeteria, they want to
be outside, in the sun. Especially now that the Garbage
Eater is gone. The cafeteria feels especially dead.

We eat. People come and go. Eventually it's just me
and Sadie sitting there.

SADIE: I had a talk with Will this morning.
ME: Why were you talking to him?
SADIE: He's having trouble with the fact that you
　　　　　and I are sort of . . . back . . .
ME: Yeah? Well, tough luck for him.
SADIE: He said he still loves me.
ME: And what did you say?
SADIE: I told him the truth.
ME: And what's that?
SADIE: That I love him, too. Or I did. You know . . .
ME: You told him *you loved him?*
SADIE: I told him I *cared* about him. It wasn't like

that. It wasn't anything. He was always very
sweet to me. I feel bad for him. I feel like
I'm . . . not being fair to him.

ME: In what way?

SADIE: He thinks maybe I liked you all along. Or
that you were waiting in the wings. I tried to
tell him it wasn't like that. It was very
unexpected.

ME: You sound like you're not that happy about it.

SADIE: I'm happy. I just . . . I know what he means.
I can see what he's saying.

ME: That reminds me of something I wanted to
ask you.

SADIE: What.

ME: About the condom.

SADIE: What about it?

ME: Where did it come from? Do you always carry a
condom in your coat pocket?

SADIE: What do you mean?

ME: I mean, you never had a condom in your
pocket when we went out.

SADIE: We were sophomores!

ME: Well, yeah, but it's still a little weird. You carry
a condom around in case you meet some guy?

SADIE: Of course not. I just think it's a good thing
to have. Someone might need it.

ME: Like who? Like your friends?

SADIE: Well, someone might . . .

ME: I was surprised. That's all. It doesn't seem like you.

SADIE: I'm sorry if it upset you.

ME: It didn't upset me. It surprised me.

SADIE: We're older now.

ME: You had sex with Will, didn't you?

SADIE (*looking at me*): Why are you asking me that?

ME: Because I want to know.

SADIE: Well, if you have to know . . . yes, I did.

ME: ——

SADIE: Is that a problem?

ME: No. But you could have told me.

SADIE: I'm sure I would have. At the right time.

ME: And when was that going to be?

SADIE: Whenever. God, look at you, you're totally freaked out about this.

ME: No, I'm not.

SADIE: Yes, you are. I can tell you are.

ME (*shaking head*): Jesus. I mean, come on. Of all the people . . .

SADIE: There's nothing wrong with Will Greer. I was very close to him. People grow up, you know.

ME: I'm sorry, but something about that doesn't seem right to me.

SADIE: As I recall, nothing about anything seems right to you. It's sort of the nature of your personality.

After the condom conversation, I feel like I need to back off. I need to regroup. Maybe I'm thinking, *I'll show Sadie.* I won't talk to her for the rest of the day. See how she likes that!

So I avoid her and I don't call her that night. Then the next day I don't look for her at school. But then about lunchtime, I totally change. I feel like I love her more than ever, and I have to forgive her. Not even forgive her — she didn't do anything wrong — but let the whole thing go. There's nothing to be done. It happened. It's over. I have to be mature about this. I have to be an adult.

The only problem is, I'm not an adult.

I end up with Gabe at Fred Meyer's after school. We wander the aisles. He picks up the nerf football and motions for me to go long. But I don't. I walk along beside him, lost in my own gloom.

That night I eat dinner at Gabe's. His mom makes the lasagna she always makes. I'm so out of it, I drop a huge chunk of it down the front of my shirt. Gabe's mom comes running to the rescue. She wets a sponge, hurries over, dabs the stain off my shirt.

She loves me, I realize. Gabe's mom *loves* me. After all the horrible things I've said about her. She loves me.

God, what's wrong with me?

Later, Renee calls Gabe and wants to know what's up. Nothing is. She and Stephanie come pick us up anyway.

Renee's got her mom's car and they wanna drive around. It's a beautiful spring night, so that seems like the thing to do. We drive around, wasting gas. I don't even care. Waste all the gas you want.

It gives me a chance to think, though. And when I get home, I call Sadie. I call her on her cell, at like midnight, and she answers. I tell her I'm sorry and I won't say anything more about her and Will.

"I'm really more worried about other things," she says.

"Like what?" I say.

"Just like, if getting back together is a good idea."

I take a breath. "It's hard, I know."

"Maybe it's too hard. And if it isn't happening naturally . . . then what's the point?"

"I know."

"And what about the summer? I'll be leaving for the eco-park at the end of June. What are you going to do? Sit around and wait for me? You'll want to do stuff, too."

"I know. I don't know about the summer."

May 18

More car issues. Dad wants me to get my car now, before summer starts. Mom wants this, too, for practical reasons. They both act like it's insane for me not to have my own vehicle. One person, one car — that's how it's supposed to work. If not, someone might be inconvenienced.

At the same time, my dad is continuing to present the car as part of a "package deal." Taking the car will mean that I will apply to college. And go. All of this makes perfect sense to my dad. College is unthinkable to him without a car. I guess that's how it was in 1979.

To me, a car seems like the last thing you need at college. That's why they *have* college, so you can rise above that crap, at least for a couple years.

My mother keeps trying to smooth things over. She thinks I'm being extreme, unrealistic, and that my resistance is all some weird resentment against Dad.

All of which is probably true.

But I also just don't want one. I don't want to put gas in it, I don't want to insure it, I don't want to park it, I don't want to look at it. If I am the first teenager in the world to refuse a car, so be it. The Garbage Eater ate tater tots off the floor.

I'm not going to own a car.

May 22

Sat with Sadie at lunch today. Things seem better
between us the last couple days. We're hanging out,
eating lunch together, joking around. It's feeling more
natural. Of course, I have begun thinking forward to the
weekend. I'm hoping we'll have sex again.

It's also been really nice out. People are walking
around in shorts and sandals. We had sixth-period social
studies outside on the main lawn, right where the
Garbage Eater used to do his Buddhist chants. We
sprawled on the grass and fell asleep as the teacher
droned on about the Three Branches of our
Representative Government.

I had the thought: The Garbage Eater fought the
administration and he is gone. I did not, and I am
still here.

So who won?

May 23

Weirdly hot today. Ninety degrees.

A bunch of seniors attempted "senior skip day" and went to the river and promptly got caught. Hard to imagine significant political upheaval from a generation that can't pull off "senior skip day."

So now they're not going to graduate unless they do some makeup class work. Everyone is up in arms about that.

I went looking for Sadie after school but she had already left. I couldn't find Gabe either, so I had to bus it home. Which sucked.

May 24

Ninety-four degrees today. A record.

People were eating outside at lunch. I sat with some other people, then Sadie and Teresa from Activist Club came and sat with us.

People were talking about the heat wave. Someone mentioned the rise in global temperatures and I joked that maybe a canned food drive would help. I was being sarcastic, of course. When I glanced over at Sadie, she gave me a brutal look.

Later, when everyone else had gone in, Sadie was still glaring at me.

"What?" I said. "I was just trying to be funny."

"If you don't respect what I do, just say so. But don't start making fun of things like the canned food drive."

"I wasn't making fun of it, I was just saying —"

"You were making fun of it."

"I didn't mean it against you —"

"I don't care how you meant it. The food drive gives food to people who are hungry."

"Okay, you're right. I shouldn't make fun of that."

We both sat there, not looking at each other.

"I have to go," she finally said, wadding up her paper lunch bag.

I watched her walk away. "Jesus," I said to myself.

*　　*　　*

After last period, I find Gabe and we walk through the
heat toward the parking lot. That's when I see two girls
standing in the loading area. There's something about
them, they stand out for some reason. We get closer. One
of them is bizarrely skinny and dressed in this strange
tube top thing. I say to Gabe, "Who is that?" Gabe
doesn't know. But as we get closer, I see who it is. It's
Tasha. The eighth grader from Sun River. In short shorts
and an eighties tube top thing that's supposed to look
sexy but looks ridiculous on her because she's fourteen
and has no body. . . .

"Hey, James!" she says, smiling like, *Isn't this the
funniest thing ever?* She cocks her hip to the side. She
does this like she's been practicing it all day in the
mirror.

"Hey," I manage to say.

Gabe looks worried. "Who is that?" he whispers.

"A girl I met on spring vacation."

"It took me a while to find you," says Tasha. She and
her friend are both chewing gum.

"Wow," I say.

"This is my friend Fiona," she says. "We got out of
school early and we were bored so we decided to come
find you."

"Wow," I say again.

She shields the sun from her eyes. "What's up?"
she says.

"Not much."

She sees then that I'm not happy to see her, that I'm not overjoyed that she is here to play the sex kitten with me. "So what are you guys doing?" she says, not giving up.

"Uh . . . ," I say. "We're just . . . Gabe and I . . . we were heading downtown —"

"What for?" she says.

"We have to . . . ," I say, trying to think of a likely story. "Go down to the skateboard store . . . Gabe has to return . . ."

Tasha's smile falters. Fiona frowns. The two of them deflate right in front of us. They were hot babes, rock stars, sex kittens, as we walked up. Now they are embarrassed eighth graders in ridiculous clothing.

"James?" I hear someone say behind me. I know who it is before I turn around.

It's Sadie.

I turn. She's coming up behind us. "Hey," she says. Then she sees who we're talking to. She stops. "Oh," she says. "Who's this?"

"This is . . . uh . . . ," I say.

"Tasha," says Tasha. "Who are you?"

"I'm Sadie." She looks at Tasha. I can see her brain working.

"She's a friend of my —" I start to say.

"No, no, that's okay," Sadie says, waving her hand. "I just wanted to talk . . . before you left. . . ."

I stare at Sadie for a moment.

"But we can talk later," she says. She turns and strides away.

"Sadie, wait."

"No," she says, walking quickly and not turning around. "That's okay, I'll call you later."

Fiona, meanwhile, is twirling her hair on her finger. "Awwwk-ward," she says.

James Hoff
Junior AP English
Mr. Cogweiller
ASSIGNMENT: *four-page essay on nature*

ON NATURE

People think of nature as something separate from us. Nature is a park, or someplace you go on vacation. But nature is all around us. It is part of us. It can help us with our problems. People don't think that but it's true.

TREES

Trees are like parents. They look down on you with a wry smile. They know how it is. Not that they're gonna cut you any slack. You still gotta do the right thing. But they're always there. No matter how bad you mess up. You can always sit beneath a tree, nurse your wounds, try to do better next time.

RIVERS

Rivers are like a talkative friend. Streams. Creeks. They babble. They make pleasing sounds. They soothe the soul. They chatter happily about nothing, allowing you to think about other things in a calming environment.

OCEANS

Oceans are more imposing. They do not sugarcoat the truth. They represent all of life, not just the fun parts. They are not terribly interested in you in particular. You are just one of many. You have a problem? So does everybody. Oceans provide humility.

THE SKY

A clear sky will swallow your problems. It will empty your brain if you let it. Gray skies are like a bad mood, dismal and heavy on your soul. The night sky is endless, full of possibilities, full of dreams you had once and forgot about. Look up. Those dreams are still there. You can always go back to them.

GRASS

Mountain grass, wild grass, grass along a trail. A place with grass is a good place to sit and think about things. Rabbits can be found in such places. Small birds. Little black bugs. Wild grass is light, airy, soft. Try not to hurt it. Try not to disturb it. Let it remind you how fragile things are.

LAKES

Lakes are still and peaceful. They are so still and peaceful you want to throw stuff into them. You throw rocks into them, sticks, logs, whatever you can find. The lake can take it. The lake can absorb all the bad energy you got. Go ahead, freak out. The lake's got all day.

RAIN

The rain comes and washes us while we sleep. It cleans our souls. It smoothes over the footprints of our mistakes. What can't the rain fix? What can't it soften and erase? The sound of it even: raindrops on your roof, raindrops on the top of a car, raindrops on the hood of your poncho when you're sitting on the curb outside your house wishing you could just once, *just once,* in your life get something right.

No matter what we do, Nature remains our protector. Even as we ignore it, contaminate it, destroy it, Nature offers us sympathy and love. It comforts us in our darkest hour. We do not deserve this. And still it is offered.

The End

May 30

Cogweiller: *These are some touching descriptions and thoughts, but it is unclear what has happened to inspire them. I can guess what has happened, but generally, that is not the reader's responsibility. Hope everything's okay.*

THE TALK

Sadie and I meet after school to have the talk. It has nothing to do with Tasha, is the first thing she says. It's not a jealousy thing. She is very careful to explain that.

We sit on the cement steps behind the art room. The conversation goes pretty smoothly. I feel like I'm gonna die when we first sit down, but once we're actually discussing things, I feel okay. There's something very ordinary about it. It's just me and Sadie talking, working stuff out, like we've done a million times before.

Her main point is that she feels like we should move forward. That we need to grow. We are so young. She loves me. She never stopped loving me. Even during her time with Will. She is glad we got together. She doesn't regret it. But summer's almost here. She is leaving for Vancouver in five weeks. She wants to go into the world unencumbered. She wants to meet people; she wants to learn, to be seventeen.

My main point is . . . well . . . I don't have a main point. I tell her I don't really like talking to anyone but her. Other people are morons. But as she points out, that is more my problem than the other people's. I'm not trying hard enough. She thinks it's ridiculous that I didn't write for the school paper this year. I would have met smart, interesting people. I would have had so much fun.

So then I bring up sex. I feel like we need to have sex

more. Or again. Or something. But she just shakes her head. I guess she already gave me as much as she can in that department. So then I say that I will miss her so much, that the last two weeks have been the best part of my whole year, of my whole life. She has no easy answer for that. She understands. She is going to miss me, too.

Then the conversation drifts off to other things. Her brother came home from Berkeley. She tells me about that. He is taking a year off. Her parents are having fits. I remember her brother. He was into techno music and gaming stuff and had long hair and was a mathematical genius. Then his parents cleaned him up and sent him off to Berkeley. Sadie says that's what you get when you try to change people. You get nothing. I agree. I wonder if I'll see him around this summer. I used to see him skateboarding sometimes. Sadie says I might.

So then we're done with our conversation. It gets hard, that part. Sadie is the first to stand up. I stand up, too, and brush the cement dust off my ass. We both look down at the baseball field where a little kid is riding his bike around the bases. I am not quite ready for this, but who is ever ready for such things? She takes my hand, squeezes it, and kisses the side of my face. She says good-bye. Then she goes inside. The big metal school door closes behind her.

I stand there. I stand there for a long time and then I sit back down where I was. It's hard sitting by myself, without her there talking to me anymore. I feel so empty.

Suddenly the world seems so utterly empty. I start to cry. Just a little, just enough to get the worst of the pain out of my chest. I wipe the snot off my face and pull myself together. Then I sit there. My knees up. My chin on my forearms. I sit there.

Endings (a short philosophical essay)

When you talk about the end of something, what do you mean? Is there ever really an end? Isn't everything always ending, all the time, everywhere, and also beginning, too?

When you break up with someone, is that the end? Don't you still have them inside you in a way?

Will the world end?

What happens when you die? Is that the end? Is there an end to the Universe?

When you empty out your locker on the last day of school, that is an end of sorts. But also the beginning of something. *Summer.* Gabe told me that Lucy Branch asked him about me. She told him that I seemed nervous during our date but she still thinks I'm cute. She asked why I don't hang out more, or go to parties or whatever. Gabe told her that I don't hang out more because I think the world is coming to an end and I'm preparing myself by locking myself in dark rooms and holding my hand over candle flames. That's Gabe's odd sense of humor. Thanks, Gabe.

Is death the end? People don't think so because they believe in heaven or reincarnation or future generations. But if we make the world uninhabitable and nothing is alive and the surface of the earth looks like the surface of Mars, wouldn't that be the end? It seems like that would be the end.

Poor Tasha. I told my sister about her showing up at my school. She said she's heard that Tasha is nuts. What is gonna happen to that girl?

When I get home, I drag my Hefty bag full of end-of-the-year crap to my room and dump it on the floor. It's pretty easy to sort out. Math stuff: trash. Biology notes: trash. Gym clothes: trash. Ragged copy of *Fahrenheit 451*: trash.

Junior year is over. That's it. The end.

June 12

Went to Safeway last night to get some stuff for my mom. Pulled in and who was getting out of the car across from me but Jill Kantor.

I'd hung out with her a couple times during the last weeks of school. Sadie had forced us together, in hopes that I'd join the school paper. Now I was embarrassed since she must have known that Sadie dumped me. Girls always know the details of that stuff. Even nerdy girls like Jill and Sadie.

But she was cool. She said hi and we walked into the store together. She talked about the paper next year and asked if I would write something for them. She said, "Didn't you write something about cars last year? Sadie told me about it. Like how we need to move beyond them?"

"You mean destroy them?" I said.

She sort of laughed, which was a good sign. She gave me her email address and told me to send it.

So when I got home, I emailed it to her. I also sent her a new thing I had called *Thoughts on Assholism*. I figured that would be the end of it. But a half hour later, she emailed back. She said she really liked both pieces.

She also asked me if I had read *21 Points for the Immediate Removal of All Corporate Influences from the Classroom*. I had to admit I had never heard of it. She said it was on this kid's website, this fifteen-year-old in Washington DC whose dad was in Congress. The website is called WastedOnTheYoung.com. He wrote all these political rants and manifestos. It had become so popular that *Time* magazine had done a profile on him. So I checked it out and it was rad! Seriously. Totally brutal and hilarious at the same time. I was kind of shocked to see someone doing something like that. It was exactly what I wanted to do. I emailed the guy immediately.

Then I emailed Jill Kantor back and thanked her and told her some other ideas I had. And she wrote back. And I wrote back. It went on like that into the night. It turned out Jill is gonna be home most of the summer. And so am I.

It made me look forward to things. Which sorta pissed me off — since that's exactly what Sadie predicted would happen if I would just open myself up a little.

I hate it when Sadie is right.

June 17

Cogweiller emailed me today. He said he's retiring from teaching and that he and his wife are moving to Arizona at the end of the summer. He wanted to stay in touch in case I needed a college recommendation from him. He said he'd be happy to write one.

I wrote him back and said thanks but I didn't think I was going to college right away. I told him I wanted to move to Washington DC after high school, and join some other people working on a website called WastedOnTheYoung.com.

I told him we hoped to engage in guerrilla media attacks, harassing people and doing funny outrageous things online to get other young people as angry and motivated as we were.

He wrote back and said, "Sounds like an adventure!" Then he gave me his mailing address just in case. I copied it down and put it in my drawer. Just in case.

APPENDIX

APPENDIX 1

"Once we were happy in our own country and we were seldom hungry, for then the two-leggeds and the four-leggeds lived together like relatives, and there was plenty for them and plenty for us. But the Wasichus [white men] came, and they made little islands for us and other little islands for the four-leggeds, and always these islands are becoming smaller, for around them surges the gnawing flood of the Wasichu; and it is dirty with lies and greed."

"That fall [1883], they say, the last of the bison herds was slaughtered by the Wasichus. I can remember when the bison were so many that they could not be counted, but more and more Wasichus came to kill them until there were only heaps of bones scattered where they used to be. The Wasichus did not kill them to eat; they killed them for the metal that makes them crazy . . . they just killed and killed because they liked to do that. When we hunted bison, we killed only what we needed. . . ."

"All our people now were settling down in square grey houses, scattered here and there across this hungry land, and around them the Wasichus had drawn a line to keep them in. The nation's hoop was broken, and there was no center any longer for the flowering tree. The people were in despair. They seemed heavy to me, heavy and dark. . . ."

"I could see that the Wasichus did not care for each other the way our people did. They would take everything from each other if they could, and so there were some who had more of everything than they could use, while crowds of people had nothing at all and maybe were starving. They had forgotten that the earth was their mother."

"I looked back in the past and recalled my people's old ways, but they were not living that way any more. They were traveling the black road, everybody for himself. . . ."

"When I look back now from this high hill of my old age, I can still see the butchered women and children lying heaped and scattered all along the crooked gulch as plain as when I saw them with eyes still young. And I can see that something else died there in the bloody mud, and was buried in the blizzard. A people's dream died there."

APPENDIX 2
FROM *The Evergreen Owl*

THOUGHTS ON ASSHOLISM
BY JAMES HOFF

I was watching one of our high school tennis matches the other day. Our best guy was playing the best guy from Wilson. The first thing I noticed was that beneath the tennis competition was a separate competition of who could be the biggest asshole.

The match was very entertaining. There was complaining, whining, arguing. Racquets were thrown. Balls were kicked. I was glad the players were indulging their assholic tendencies. Assholes are more fun to watch than people who keep their cool. Assholes are more fun in general, as long as they're not being assholes to you.

In our society, we teach young people to be modest and humble, to respect authority. The people who absorb this message tend to be the people who are humble anyway: the dorks, the losers, people who wear glasses. These people nod knowingly when adults explain that assholism hurts others and leads to personal unhappiness. They agree. They think being quiet and meek is the better way to go. That is convenient since that is how they are anyway.

Meanwhile, the assholes hear this message and laugh. They already know the reality of American life: Assholes rule! Being meek gets you nothing! Get out there and grab whatever you can, fight for it, kill for it! If one of these assholes happens to meet another asshole trying to get the same thing, well, now things get interesting. Now we have free market competition! Everyone loves a good fight. Even the dorks and losers can be roused from their video games to watch the assholes duke it out.

The tennis players spat a lot. They stalked around the court scowling at each other. They didn't just want to win, they wanted to screw the other guy over. People could feel the assholism and soon a large crowd gathered. Both these tennis players probably get millions of girls.

We are taught the greatness of the Dalai Lama, Mother Teresa, Martin Luther King. But who do we really stand in awe of? Not those people. We prefer winners, conquerors, the rich, the famous. We love athletes who crush their opponents. We like companies who strangle their competition. When our politicians steal elections, we stand in awe, unable to act, we're so mesmerized by this extreme and fascinating assholity. We respect people with the *cojones* to screw other people over. We love the victorious. We don't care how they did it. The more ruthless the better.

"But what does this mean in our current situation as we stand at the brink of ecological disaster?" you ask.

As long as there were relatively few of us and we didn't have the technology to do serious harm to our surroundings, we could pretty much do whatever we wanted to each other. Cheat, murder, blackmail, behead. If this was our idea of fun, whatever. We were only hurting ourselves.

Now, though, our love of assholism has consequences. Certain people will make billions of dollars from the oil that is still in the ground. We could possibly save the planet if we left it there and found other forms of energy. But those people don't want that to happen. They want their billions, and they don't mind screwing us over to get it.

Meanwhile we stand in awe, as usual. We think: They're not really going to ruin the earth for all future generations, are they? Just for a little more money? They would endanger all living things? They wouldn't do that. Nobody is that much of an asshole.

But they would do it. And they will.

Which is why, fellow dorks, losers, and people who wear glasses, this might be a good time to pry yourself away from the computer games....

APPENDIX 3

FROM *wastedontheyoung.com/college-applications*

THE ART OF THE COLLEGE APPLICATION: THE PERSONAL ESSAY
BY JAMES HOFF

First of all, I would like to thank the college admissions board for the opportunity to share with you some of the special qualities that I hope to bring to your excellent institution. As you can see, I am pretty much exactly what you are looking for. For instance:

1. I AM A MAJOR LEAGUE SUCK UP. I really am. I like you. I like your college. I want to learn from you. I think spending four years with you will be the best thing that has ever happened to me. Your influence will change me forever. I can't wait to grow up and be like you in every way.

2. I AM A REGURGITATION MACHINE. On papers or tests, I don't like to think too much. Thinking sometimes leads to conclusions that don't get you an A. I like to remember what my teacher thought and write that down instead. That usually leads to a more positive outcome.

3. I PLAY IT SAFE. I never do weird things. I don't even sing in the shower. What if my college counselor was walking by and she heard me singing incorrectly and she mentioned on my college applications that I can't sing? How would I get into the best college and get the best job and make the most money, with such a mark on my record?

4. I ONLY LIKE WHAT I'M SUPPOSED TO LIKE. You know that cool new band everyone is talking about? I don't. That's because I don't pay attention to current trends. Why should I? They haven't passed the test of time. I know that Bob Dylan is good because adults tell me so. Even though he can't sing and his songs go on forever and he sounds like he has a clothespin pinching his nose, Mr. Dylan is *established.*

5. I HAVE DONE EVERYTHING RIGHT. Many people think your teen years are a time to experiment, take risks, and discover who you really are. Me, I've focused on being perfect. I have memorized my textbooks, never questioned my teachers, and spent all my free time doing pointless, non-threatening extracurriculars like Statistics Club and JV Badminton. After college, I plan to work for a multinational corporation and exploit poor people for my own financial gain. If anyone says I have done something wrong, I will say, "On the contrary, I have done everything right!"

6. NO CHANGES FOR ME. As long as everything stays like it is, I will get a high-powered job, make tons of money, and will live in a huge house protected by iron gates. For this reason I don't want to change anything. When people say we need to rethink our unsustainable lifestyle, I say, "Oh yeah? And what's *your* grade point average?" When they say we have to stop plundering the earth and polluting the air, I say, "Excuse me, but that's my parking space." Admitting me to your fine institution will help everything stay the same. And isn't that what we all really want?

APPENDIX 4
FROM *Black Elk Speaks*

"Now and then [Crazy Horse] would . . . have the crier call me into his tepee to eat with him. Then he would say things to tease me, but I wouldn't say anything back because I think I was a little afraid of him. I was not afraid he would hurt me; I was just afraid. Everybody felt that way about him, for he was a queer man and would go about the village without noticing people or saying anything. In his own tepee he would joke, and when he was on the warpath with a small party he would joke to make his warriors feel good. But around the village he hardly ever noticed anybody, except little children. All the Lakotas like to dance and sing but he never joined a dance, and they say nobody ever saw him sing. But everybody liked him, and they would do anything he wanted or go anywhere he said. He was a small man among the Lakotas and he was slender and had a thin face and his eyes looked through things and he always seemed to be thinking about something. He never wanted to have many things for himself, and did not have many ponies like a chief. They say that when game was scarce and the people were hungry, he would not eat at all. He was a queer man. Maybe he was always part way into that world of his vision. He was a very great man, and I think if the

Wasichus had not murdered him down there, maybe we should still have the Black Hills and be happy. They could not kill him in battle. They had to lie to him and murder him. And he was only about thirty years old when he died."